MUSLIMAH MUKALLAF

THE MUSLIMAHS GUIDE TO PUBERTY, FAITH, AND PERSONAL CARE

JENNA BINT HAKEEM

Paperback ISBN: 979-8-218-45368-8

Cover design and typography by Jenna bint Hakeem
Illustrated by Jenna bint Hakeem
Edited by Sanjana Verma

Printed in the United States of America
First Printing Edition: 2024
www.jennabinthakeem.com

Contents

Asalaamu'alaykum dear reader, welcome to Muslimah Mukallaf.

From the moment you were born, you've been loved and cared for by your parents and caretakers. They've fed you, clothed you, shared valuable lessons, and raised you with deep tenderness and thought. For a while, you didn't have to think about who you are or what your future holds. You didn't have to think about how to be a Muslim or what it actually means to be one. As a child, your parents guided your every step, taking on all responsibilities so you could freely explore and enjoy your childhood. However, your life won't be like this forever; after all, Puberty is on its way.

Imagine, one night, you go to sleep, your head resting peacefully on the pillow, a mind free from any deep concerns; the next, you are growing taller, body parts are changing, your smell is different, and hair pops up in places that aren't on your head. You start to notice how you look, wonder who you are, and what your place is, in this big, wide world. Then, all of a sudden, you find red stains in your underwear.

Congratulations, you are now Mukallaf! From this moment on, taking care of your changing body, praying, fasting, and even wearing hijaab have now become obligatory for you. Your beliefs, actions, and decisions are now your own to make in the sight of Allaah.

However, there's still much to learn. Sometimes, we might be too shy to ask our parents about things we ought to know. Other times, we might get information online or from a friend that isn't accurate or doesn't paint a complete picture. Often, we learn about the general practices of being a Muslim without understanding the specifics for women and girls, like menstrual care, how to wear hijaab, and keeping clean.

That's where I come in. I have written this book for you, dear reader, so that it may guide you through this new and uncharted chapter of your life. As a young woman myself, I was in your shoes only a few years ago. I get what it's like to not know what's happening inside while life is evolving and everything is brand new. As your older sister in Islaam, it's my duty to pass the knowledge of navigating Puberty down to you.

This book has everything from body changes and menstrual care to overwhelming feelings, new Islaamic duties, and even beauty and styling tips. It is for every young Muslimah trying to learn about her body, religious obligations, and personal care.

As a growing girl, you must have many questions that need answers. So, without further delay, let's start this journey together.

- Your loving sister, Jenna bint Hakeem

Part One
PUBERTY & HYGIENE

PUBERTY AND WHAT TO EXPECT

Puberty is the process of your body changing from girl to woman. From your mother to the mothers of the believers, this experience connects you to all women worldwide since the beginning of time! Allaah created your body to grow and mature so you will be prepared for natural life. Many changes during Puberty are meant to prepare you for potential motherhood later on, while others are to keep your body healthy, mature your mind, and enable you to fulfill your life's purpose.

During this process of growing up, you'll notice your relationships with friends and family changing into something new, your heart will feel things more intensely than ever before, and how you look begins to matter as you adapt to your new body.

At the same time, this process allows you to discover more about yourself, the world, and other people. It enables you to become closer to Allaah, make meaningful relationships, experience precious moments, and form sweet memories on your journey to womanhood. It isn't as crazy as the movies make it out to be, but it isn't a piece of cake either. Enjoy the process, and prepare yourself with knowledge to make this transition all the more pleasant.

WHAT DOES IT MEAN TO BE MUKALLAF?

It was narrated by Ali ibn Abi Taalib that the Messenger of Allaah ﷺ said, "The pen is lifted from three people: a sleeping person until he awakens, a child until he reaches puberty, and an insane person until he regains his sanity." - [at-Tirmidhi]

This Hadeeth teaches us that we are not held accountable for our actions in three conditions. The first is when sleeping, the second is before Puberty, and the third is if you are not sane.

This means that the person who is Mukallaf (accountable for their actions) has reached Puberty and is of sound mind.

Whatever Allaah has commanded in the Quraan and Sunnah is now obligatory for you, and whatever Allaah has forbidden in the Quraan and Sunnah is now Haraam for you.

WHEN WILL PUBERTY HAPPEN TO ME?

Puberty begins when your brain's hormones (your body's chemical messaging system) start producing estrogen. Estrogen is the hormone responsible for feminine characteristics in the body, such as your menstrual cycle, egg production, breast growth, and other parts of your development.

Other hormones from the adrenal glands on top of your kidneys produce further Puberty symptoms, like body odor, pubic hair, and acne.
Puberty doesn't happen overnight. It is a gradual process that can happen between the ages of eight and thirteen and usually lasts between two to five years. There are a few common signs of Puberty that each girl experiences in different variations.

Remember, everyone is unique, and Puberty happens differently for each person. Some girls see changes as early as eight, nine, or ten years old, while others begin later, around thirteen or fourteen. Some girls skip a few of these signs, while others experience all of them. Sometimes years go by without you having a particular symptom, and suddenly, it comes in full swing. Let your body develop at its own pace, and don't worry if you haven't experienced some of these signs yet. Insha Allaah, they will come when Allaah decides you're ready.

WHAT ARE THE SIGNS OF PUBERTY?

Although ten signs are listed here, only three of them make you Mukallaf. Be sure to pay attention to find out which ones they are. This is only a brief explanation for each sign in no particular order, and most will be discussed in detail with their very own chapters.

DISCHARGE

Discharge is a clear, white, or yellowish fluid that might remind you of snot from a runny nose. It comes out of your private area every day, sometimes a little, and sometimes a lot. This discharge is part of your body's natural way of keeping itself clean and fighting off infections in the urinary tract. Vaginal discharge is often one of the earliest signs of Puberty.

NEW BODY ODORS

During Puberty, your hormones become more active, causing your glands (cells that release things your body needs) to produce more sweat. Sweating is a normal and healthy process, but once that sweat mixes with certain bacteria on your skin, it causes an odor, especially in your armpits.

But there's no need to worry. This just means it's time to start being extra mindful about cleanliness and using deodorant daily to prevent unpleasant scents.

BREASTS

As you grow, so will your chest. At first, the raised bud (called the nipple) and the areola (the darker circle around the nipple) might lie flat against your chest. But as you grow, a breast bud will start to appear. During this process, your chest may feel a little tender and sore, which is totally normal—it's just your body developing for the first time.

Breasts are made of glands and fat that prepare your body for the possibility of feeding a baby in the future. They don't always grow in the same shape or size as each other, and as breasts develop, the nipple and areola may also change shape.

Remember that breasts take a long time to fully develop and do not stop growing until age twenty-five! Yes, they take a long time to grow and completely shape, so be patient and thankful, and have pride in the beautiful body Allaah gave you as it grows.

PUBIC HAIR - A SIGN YOU ARE MUKALLAF

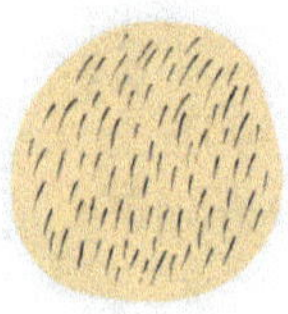

During Puberty, besides the tiny body hairs that grow on your legs, arms, and stomach, you will find that even thicker and longer hairs begin growing in your armpits and private area.

This is called pubic hair, which protects your sensitive areas from irritation and infection. It is also one of the three signs that you're Mukallaf.

MENSES - A SIGN YOU ARE MUKALLAF

One of the most anticipated signs of Puberty is the start of your menstrual cycle, also known as getting your period, or your menses. This is one of the three signs that you've become Mukallaf.

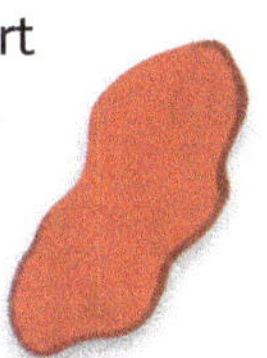

During your menses, drops of blood flow out of your private area for around five to seven days. This process is part of your built-in reproductive system (your body's system for growing and birthing a baby later on).

You may need to take extra care of yourself during your menses since it will probably come with other symptoms like cramps or acne. During your menses, there are certain acts of worship you can't do until it's over.

After you get your first period, it will come once a month, Insha Allaah, except in cases when you become very sick, pregnant, or reach the age where it's no longer possible for you to give birth.

ACNE

Acne occurs when your pores (the tiny openings in your skin that produce oils and hairs) become clogged with dirt, dead skin, and oil, which results in red bumps, pimples, blackheads, whiteheads, and dark spots. Acne can show up on your face, back, and shoulders. During Puberty, you may get a heightened amount of acne because your hormones are going crazy preparing you for adulthood. Acne can also flare up on your menses, when you're stressed, using bad soaps, being unclean, or not eating well.

CELLULITE

Cellulite is what happens when your body stores fat around your thigh area under the skin's surface. This is a common thing that most women and girls have and usually isn't noticeable or cause for concern. Each body needs a healthy amount of fat storage for growth and as a reserve for potential pregnancy or times of food scarcity. If you're not getting enough nutrients, your body will use this stored fat to keep you going. AlHamdulillaah, Allaah gave your body so many ways to keep you safe and healthy. This also depends on your genetics, so if someone in your family has cellulite, you might get it too.

GROWTH SPURTS AND STRETCH MARKS

During Puberty, you'll likely go through a growth spurt where you experience a rapid increase in height. Sometimes, when your body grows faster than your skin can keep up with, you might develop stretch marks on your thighs, hips, and other places. Not everyone gets these, and they often go away on their own with time.

HEIGHTENED EMOTION

During Puberty, your hormones are working overtime to help you grow into a healthy young woman. This not only affects your physical body, but your mind, too. Suddenly, feelings like anger, sadness, and worry are more intense when something triggers them.

Things you didn't care about before are now sensitive topics for you, and it's easy to get upset, feel deeply sad, or become overwhelmed by stress. You might start feeling self-conscious about your body, question parts of your personality, or be hard on yourself over small mistakes.As Muslims, we know that Shaytaan and his helpers also prey on negative emotions to make them worse and lead us to unhealthy ways of coping.

The good news is, your capacity for happiness, love, and care also grows during Puberty. You'll learn so much about yourself and the world around you, and with practice, you will be able to manage and nurture your overwhelming feelings for the better. This season of intense emotion is only temporary and will even out on its own as your mind and body settle into adulthood.

WET DREAMS - A SIGN YOU ARE MUKALLAF

Remember when we spoke about discharge earlier? Well, when your imagination drifts to certain romantic scenarios, you may feel a tingling sensation in your private area which causes a higher amount of discharge to flow.

This is a natural feeling and is part of your body's reproductive system, but remember, engaging in these feelings should wait until marriage, a topic we'll cover later on Insha Allaah.

A wet dream is what happens when you dream about romantic intimacy and wake up with a lot of discharge in your underwear. In Islaam, discharge caused by a wet dream or romantic intimacy is called maniy. This is one of the three signs that you have become Mukallaf.

If you have a wet dream, don't be embarrassed. Just make sure to take a ghusl (a type of bath that will be explained in a later chapter) when you wake up. This puts you back into a purified state so you'll be able to pray.

WHAT IF I DON'T DEVELOP ANY OF THESE SIGNS?

Remember, it's okay to be a late bloomer. Maybe you didn't get your menses this year, but your chest is growing, and so is your body hair. Perhaps you have your menses and nothing else is physically happening, but your feelings are all over the place. Maybe you think you'll never get acne, but you wake up with it after two years of going through Puberty. Maybe you worry about feeling down forever, but then one day, your skin clears up and you're in a bright mood that becomes your norm for the rest of your life.

Be patient and thankful for your body by taking care of it. Puberty doesn't follow the same schedule for everyone, and that's perfectly okay.

However, if you haven't seen any signs of Puberty by age thirteen, it's a good idea to see a doctor and make sure everything is progressing as it should inside. At the same time, if you don't get your menses, pubic hair, or have any wet dreams during the listed Puberty years, you will still automatically become Mukallaf at age fifteen.

CARING FOR YOUR BODY INSIDE

Human beings come in all shapes, sizes, colors, and features, each uniquely beautiful in their own special way. Not only is your body on the outside a wonderful blessing from Allaah, but the inside that keeps you functioning, such as your heart, mind, lungs, stomach, uterus, and kidneys, shows just how much of a gift it is from our Creator.

This is why you must understand the importance of caring for your body, not only by keeping it clean but ensuring it stays healthy from the inside. Especially during Puberty, when your body navigates the transition from girl to woman, it requires extra attention and care.

In Islaam, we're taught many practices to keep ourselves healthy. Carrying them out is a way of thanking Allaah for this incredible gift.

Have you ever gotten a cold that stuffed up your nose, and you could only breathe through your mouth? Suddenly, because the ability was taken from you, you realize how much of a blessing it is to be able to breathe freely. Having good health is a blessing often overlooked and sometimes only recognized when it's taken away.

It was narrated by Ibn `Abbaas that the Prophet ﷺ said: "There are two blessings that many of the people squander: health and free time." - [al-Bukhaari]

On the day of judgment, you will be asked about the blessings Allaah has given you, including your health.

Abu Hurairah narrated that the Messenger of Allaah ﷺ said: "Indeed the first of what will be asked about on the Day of Judgment, is that it will be said to him: 'Did We not make your body, health, and give you of cool water to drink?'" - [at-Tirmidhi]

So, dear reader, don't wait until you're unhealthy to take care of your body and thank Allaah for it. If you keep yourself healthy, you'll be strong enough to go through Puberty with ease, do many good deeds, and have a better quality of life. By looking after your body for the sake of Allaah, you'll gain so many extra blessings. How wonderful is that?

HOW DO I KEEP MY BODY HEALTHY?

STAYING ACTIVE AND EXERCISING

Staying active is crucial for maintaining good physical health. It keeps bones and muscles nice and strong, gives you energy for every day activities, and even improves mental health and brain power. This is because exercise releases chemicals like endorphins and serotonin, which lift your mood, reduce stress, make you feel good, and help you sleep well.

If you find yourself out of breath, tired, and sluggish during everyday chores, climbing stairs, or small amounts of playtime, this is a sign you are unfit and need to strengthen your bones and muscles by staying active.

Everyone should get at least two and a half hours of exercise weekly. To keep your body healthy and strong, you can take walks, run, ride a bike, jump rope, swim, or follow ten—to fifteen-minute beginner exercise videos.

Health isn't defined by having visible abs or being skinny; it's about feeling good inside and managing daily activities easily without becoming tired and out of breath. If this describes you, you're on the right track to being a fit and healthy young woman with nothing to worry about.

In Islaam, we are taught to stay active and avoid laziness. This is not only to strengthen our bodies but our minds as well. Let's say you spend your days laying in bed, sitting on the couch, and only moving for small chores, to get food, or to go in and out of rooms. This will cause you to lose motivation, easily fall into negative moods, procrastinate, miss prayers, not take care of yourself, or put effort into bettering your life.

In fact, in the Du'aa against depression, we find that the Prophet ﷺ not only asks Allaah's protection from sadness but also laziness since it can become a habit that contributes to a persistently negative mood.

With this in mind, remember that over-exercising isn't good for you either and can actually do the opposite, weakening your body instead of keeping you healthy. Unless your doctor says your weight is causing health risks, exercising beyond thirty minutes to an hour daily can be excessive.

Exercising should leave you feeling energized and uplifted, not exhausted, weak, or deflated. If you have an intense workout routine, taking one or two rest days is important so you don't overwork your body and burn out. You should only do intensive workouts if your doctor says your weight is causing health risks. In such cases, do not go online and accept any random workout; instead, ask your doctor for a healthy routine that suits your specific needs and health goals.

EATING WELL

Food is a wonderful gift from Allaah. He placed plants and animals on earth to give us the nutrients we need for a healthy and good quality of life. Your responsibility, dear reader, is to fill your body with foods that will energize and nourish you.

If you constantly feel unmotivated, sluggish, or unable to focus, you're likely not eating well. **Even the skinniest people can be unhealthy by choosing foods that lack nutrients and harm their bodies rather than nurture them.** This issue often stems from unhealthy eating habits.

Sometimes, we might not be hungry but still eat because we're bored, sad, or just crave something that tastes good.

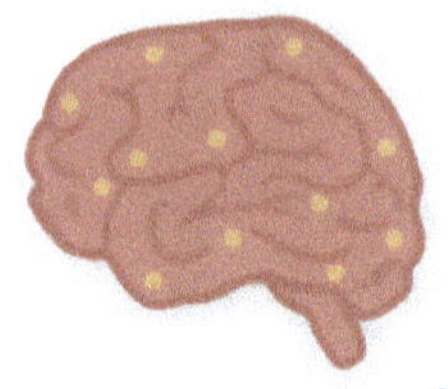

Eating for comfort, pleasure, and boredom are signs of unhealthy eating habits. Instead of eating for energy and nutrients, you're eating for pleasure. **Pleasure eating makes you choose overly sweet, salty, and fattening foods because they comfort your brain for a little while.** This comfort comes from dopamine, a chemical your brain releases that makes you feel good and affects your mood, memory, learning ability, and sleep.

Pleasure eating also makes you overeat because you're already full, and keep eating anyway for comfort. But the feeling is temporary because after the overeating is done, you feel weak, sluggish, tired, have gained unnecessary weight, and your mind is no longer as sharp. **This is why you should choose foods that nourish your body instead of only giving temporary comfort.**

Finally, pleasure eating can cause a food addiction because your brain can become addicted to the dopamine rush from eating certain foods. That's why we must question if we're truly hungry before eating. Ask yourself, Is my stomach really empty? If so, eat. But if your stomach is fine and your brain is just thinking about food, needing a distraction, or comfort for stress, sadness, or a hard day, choose something else to keep busy or deal with your feelings in a healthier way. Of course, it's okay to enjoy the food you eat. Just make sure to eat it when you are actually hungry, and make better choices that are both yummy and good for you.

Remember that junk food often gives head and stomach aches, makes you feel sluggish and sick, and affects your ability to remember, focus, or understand things. It destroys your teeth, makes your immune system weak, and causes unhealthy weight gain, food addiction, diabetes, and other diseases.

Replace junk snacks with healthier alternatives. Instead of chips, candy, ice cream, and soda, choose popcorn, yogurt, fruits, nuts, berries, and Vimto with ice or sparkling water. For more healthier snack replacements, look online and choose what looks most delicious to you.

WHAT ARE HEALTHY EATING HABITS?

It is a common misconception that eating well means eating until you're full. Whenever you eat, it should be for energy, not to fill your stomach, as explained in this Hadeeth:

> **Miqdam bin Madikarib said: "I heard the Messenger of Allaah ﷺ say, 'A human being fills no worse vessel than his stomach. It is sufficient for a human being to eat a few mouthfuls to keep his spine straight. But if he must (fill it), then one third of food, one third for drink and one third for air.'" - [Ibn Maajah]**

Here, our Prophet ﷺ teaches us that the worst thing to fill is our stomachs. You must eat enough to give you energy for daily activity and stop there. He then splits the stomach space into three parts, explaining that one part should be filled with food, one should be filled with drink, and the rest should be left for air. Eat when you are hungry, and implement this method to keep your food intake balanced.

If, according to your doctor, your weight is threatening your health, this practice should allow you to lose and manage your excess weight over time, especially if you're keeping active. But no matter your size, this practice is crucial for maintaining a healthy body instead of becoming sick and weak from your food.

It is the Sunnah to fast on Mondays and Thursdays or three days each month on the thirteenth, fourteenth, and fifteenth.

> **Aisha narrated that: "The Prophet ﷺ was keen to fast on Mondays and Thursdays." - [at-Tirmidhi]**

> **Jareer ibn' Abd-Allaah narrated that the Prophet ﷺ said: "Fasting three days of each month is fasting for a lifetime, and ayyam al-beed (the white days) are the thirteenth, fourteenth and fifteenth." - [an-Nasaa'i]**

If you choose to follow this Sunnah, be sure to fast correctly by having a suhoor of lots of water and dates to keep you hydrated and strong, staying active with worship, avoiding sleeping the day away, breaking fast with dates and lots of water, and keeping with the one third rule in your stomach for iftaar. This will give you the best results of fasting, both spiritually and for losing unhealthy weight over time.

Avoid too much red meat, like beef, lamb, goat, etc, and eat poultry, like chicken, turkey, duck, and fish, instead. Eating foods mentioned in the

Quraan and Sunnah, such as dates, barley, watermelon, olives, honey, water, and milk, will give you much nutrition and keep you healthy.

WHAT NUTRIENTS DOES YOUR BODY NEED EVERY DAY?

To keep yourself healthy, you must eat from all seven food groups every day. This way, your body gets everything it needs.

Carbohydrates give you energy, help control blood sugar, and release chemicals that help your body function. Carbohydrates are in grains like rice, oatmeal, pasta, and other foods like dates, apples, bananas, potatoes, corn, kidney, and garbanzo beans.

Proteins support your body in controlling your muscle movement, cells, and the chemical processes that help your body function. Proteins are found in foods like beef, lamb, goat, seafood, dairy products, chicken, eggs, and fish.

Fats fuel your body and act as an energy storage when you really need them. They prevent organs from going into shock and heat loss in extreme cold. Fats also help us absorb essential vitamins. Fats can be found in beef, lamb, goat, chicken, fatty fish, olive oil, yogurt, eggs, cheese, and certain seeds.

Vitamins help your fingernails, hair, and body grow. They also boost your immune system to protect against sickness, strengthen your bones, and help regulate your hormones. Vitamins can be found in all types of food, so you won't have to take them separately unless your doctor says you need to.

Minerals are a group of many nutrients that keep your brain, organs, and bones functioning. They also make hormones and help with nerve and muscle function. Minerals are found in foods such as meat, fish, milk, fruits, vegetables, nuts, and cereals.

Fiber stabilizes your blood sugar, prevents constipation, helps maintain a healthy weight, and keeps your digestive system healthy. Fibers are found in fruits, vegetables, nuts, and whole grains like cereal and oatmeal.

Water is essential for keeping your body healthy and running smoothly. It gives you energy, heightens brain function, regulates body temperature, rids your body of waste, helps with weight loss, prevents constipation and headaches, and lubricates your joints and mouth. **It is recommended that girls between the ages of 9-18 drink 5-8 cups of water per day; the older you are, the more you'll need.**

Although cold water does taste better, it makes it harder to digest food and can make your stomach feel strange. If you are on your menses, cold water can worsen your cramps. Drinking water that's room temperature or a little warm is better because it not only helps with digestion but also blood circulation.

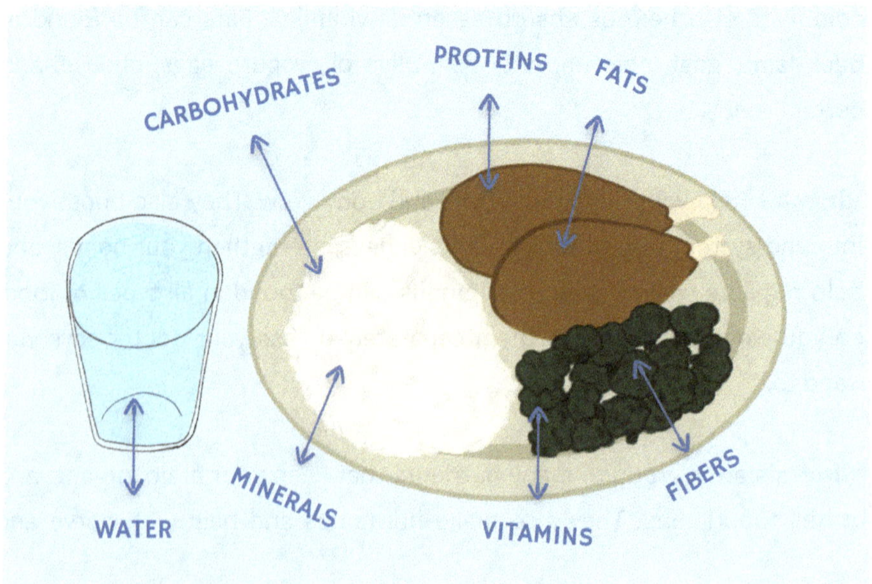

Ever heard the phrase, "You are what you eat"? This expression means that whatever you put into your body will affect how you feel and act. For example, eating greasy, heavy, and unhealthy foods will make you tired, sluggish, and unmotivated. Eating light, nourishing, and healthy foods makes you feel full of energy and ready to take on whatever the day brings.

Since we are His creation, Allaah knows us best and has given us guidelines on what foods we can and cannot eat to benefit our bodies. Halaal foods are everything except what Allaah mentions as being Haraam.

> **"So eat from the good, lawful things which Allaah has provided for you, and be grateful for Allaah's favors, if you (truly) worship Him (alone)." - [Quraan, 16:114]**

HARAAM FOODS

Alcohol is poisonous, intoxicating, and addictive. You cannot pray while intoxicated, as you are not in a sane state of mind, and alcohol is made of ingredients that are poisonous to the body.

> **"Oh you who believe! Intoxicants, gambling, idols, and drawing lots for decisions are all evil of Shaytaan's handiwork. So shun them so you may be successful." - [Quraan, 5:9]**

Pork (pig meat) can put you at risk for heart disease, obesity, high blood pressure, and stroke. Humans can also contract viruses and infections from pig meat.

Blood can contain harmful and poisonous bacteria. You can contract many diseases from drinking blood, and the human body cannot digest it.

Carrion (Animals who were dead before you found them and now have decaying flesh) is extremely dangerous because once the animal dies, the body begins releasing toxins, which will cause food poisoning and could be lethal.

Animals killed in the name of other than Allaah are also Haraam for us. When choosing what to eat, you must think about where it came from and the spiritual purity of the food. If an animal was slaughtered for the sake of a God other than Allaah, you are allowing something that was prepared with shirk (worshipping other than and associating partners with Allaah) into your body.

When slaughtered, the animal's energy greatly affects how you feel when eating it, which is why the Halaal process for slaughtering an animal is so specific. Muslims must keep their body and energies pure to worship Allaah alone; this includes watching what you eat.

> **"He has only forbidden you (to eat) carrion, blood, swine, and what is slaughtered in the name of any other than Allaah. But if someone is compelled by necessity—neither driven by desire nor exceeding immediate need—then surely Allaah is All-Forgiving, Most Merciful." - [Quraan, 16:114]**

It is not only Haraam to eat and drink these things on their own, but also if they are mixed with other foods. For example, Gelatin is an ingredient that comes from boiling pig parts and is often used in candy to give it a chewy texture. Because it's mixed with pork ingredients, that candy is now Haraam to eat. The same rule applies to foods cooked with alcohol and so on.

WHAT MAKES MEAT HALAAL?

Halaal meat comes from when an animal is raised in a clean, non-abusive, or stressful environment and is slaughtered with a sharp knife to its jugular in the name of Allaah. This is the best way to kill an animal, as it allows them to feel the least amount of pain for a short period of time and drain the most blood, which is healthier for us to eat.

This way of slaughtering animals also keeps them spiritually pure, so when we eat its meat, it won't negatively affect our mood or Imaan. Instead, it will give us energy and make us feel thankful and closer to Allaah.

Food from the people of the book (Christians and Jews) is also Halaal to eat, since they uphold similar practices as us when it comes to slaughtering.

> **"Made lawful to you this day are At-Tayyibat. The food of the People of the Scripture is lawful to you, and your food is lawful to them..." - [Quraan, 5:5]**

SLEEPING WELL

A good night's sleep is essential for staying healthy. If you don't sleep well, you might find it hard to focus, feel sluggish throughout the day, and be easily irritable or moody. Sleep is a time for your body to grow, your mind to rest, and your skin to refresh. It also helps you stay healthy and fight off sickness and disease.

A consistent sleep schedule is important so your body knows when to wind down. **If you're between 10-18 years old, getting a total of 9-10 hours of sleep every night is recommended.**

Keep active throughout the day, and get enough exercise so you will be tired when it's time for bed. Otherwise, falling asleep might take a while since your body has yet to wear out.

Taking a warm shower or bath and changing into pajamas can help you start to feel sleepy. Do your nighttime skincare or haircare routine, and turn your electronic devices off an hour before bed so your mind won't be so active. Read a book or some Quraan to calm your mind. Make sure you've prayed Ishaa, and before closing your eyes, take a moment to ask Allaah for forgiveness, thank Him for all your blessings, and offer many Du'aas before sleeping. This can help your heart and mind feel at peace as you drift off to sleep.

THE SUNNAH OF SLEEPING

It is the Sunnah to be in wudhoo before bed and to sleep on your right side, as mentioned in this Hadeeth:

> **Al-Bara' bin' Azib narrated that: "The Messenger of Allaah ﷺ directed me thus: 'Whenever you go to bed, perform wudhoo as you do for Salaah, and lie on your right side'"... - [al-Bukhaari]**

It is the Sunnah to dust off your bed before sleep with the bottom of your night clothing inside out, getting rid of any dirt and dead skin that may be left on your sheets, then to say the Du'aa in the following Hadeeth.

Abu Huraira narrated that the Prophet ﷺ said: "When anyone of you goes to bed, he should dust it off thrice with the edge of his garment, and say: With Your Name my Lord, I lay myself down and with Your Name I rise. And if my soul You take, forgive it, and if You send it back then protect it as You protect Your righteous slaves." - [al-Bukhaari]

You should also recite the three quls (Suratul Ikhlaas, Falaq, and Naas) into your Du'aa hands, then lightly and dryly spit into them and wipe them over your body from head to toe. Do this three times, as explained here:

Aisha narrated that: "When the Prophet ﷺ went to his bed every night, he would put his cupped hands together, then blow (spit lightly and drily into them), then recite into them the last three surahs of the Quraan, then he would wipe his hands over as much of his body as he could, starting with his head and face, and the front part of his body. He would do that three times." - [al-Bukhaari]

Finally, you should also recite Ayatul-Kursi before sleep for protection against Shaytaan during the night.

Abu Huraira narrated that: "The Messenger of Allaah ﷺ put me in charge of guarding the collected zakaah of Ramadhaan. Someone came and started to rummage in the food. I took hold of him and said, I will surely take you to the Messenger of Allaah ﷺ... He [the one who rummaged in the food] said, When you go to your bed, recite Ayatul-Kursi and you will be protected by Allaah, and no devil will come near you until morning. The Prophet ﷺ said, 'He told you the truth even though he is a liar. That was a devil.'" - [al-Bukhaari]

The general Du'aa for sleeping as well as waking up is mentioned here:

> **Hudhayfah ibn al-Yaman said: "When the Prophet ﷺ wanted to sleep, he would say, 'Bismika Allaahumma amutu wa ahya (In your name, Oh Allaah, I die and I live)', and when he woke up he would say 'Al-hamdu Lillah alladhi ahyana ba'da ma amatana wa ilayhi al-nushur (Praise be to Allaah who has brought us back to life after causing us to die, and to Him is the resurrection).'" - [al-Bukhaari]**

All of these Sunnahs protect you from Shaytaan messing with you in your sleep and in your dreams; they allow you to go to bed in the remembrance of Allaah and with His protection.

Our Prophet ﷺ taught us to sleep on our right side, which is good for your heart, digestion, and back pain. Although it is not the Sunnah, sleeping on your back and left side is allowed. However, sleeping on your stomach is Makrooh (disliked by Allaah).

> **It was narrated from Qais bin Tihfah Al-Ghifari that his father said: "The Messenger of Allaah ﷺ found me sleeping in the masjid on my stomach. He nudged me with his foot and said: 'Why are you sleeping like this? This is a kind of sleep that Allaah hates.'" - [Ibn Maajah]**

Just as sleeping too little isn't good for you, sleeping too much also causes health issues. Sleeping more than needed might make you feel sluggish, sad, or depressed. It's also been linked to health issues like diabetes, heart problems, and obesity. When it comes to sleep, it's all about balance.

Finally, after Dhuhr in the afternoon, it's the Sunnah to take a short nap, as said in the following Hadeeth.

Taking a short nap during the day helps improve your mood and even makes learning easier. It lowers blood pressure and makes up for any sleep you may have missed at night. Although it isn't specified in the Sunnah, it's recommended that your midday nap be between thirty minutes to an hour and a half. This way, you can wake up feeling refreshed without affecting your sleep at night.

KEEPING CLEAN AND SMELLING GOOD

Cleanliness is part of being a Muslim. After accepting Islaam, the first thing a person must learn is how to keep clean, or else their worship may not be accepted. Our Prophet Muhammad ﷺ cared a lot about having good hygiene, looking presentable, and smelling good.

Abu Malik al-Ash'ari narrated that the Messenger of Allaah ﷺ said: "Cleanliness is half of faith..." - [Sahih Muslim]

As you enter Puberty, you'll notice your body odor change and grow stronger. This is because your sweat glands become more active, and new chemicals are released to help you develop and mature.

It's important, dear reader, to take your hygiene seriously. Not only is keeping clean part of worship, but it also says a lot about who you are and how people will perceive you.

If your breath stinks, people will avoid talking to you so they don't have to smell it. If your armpits are musty, people might think you don't wash and feel uncomfortable around you. If you don't properly clean yourself after using the restroom, your scent will offend others and can earn you an embarrassing reputation.

On the other hand, if your breath is fresh and your smile is bright, people will enjoy talking to you. If you smell pleasant and clean, others will feel comfortable around you. They might even ask how you smell so good and enjoy your company even more. Remember, caring for your hygiene is caring for yourself and respecting those around you.

HOW DO I PREVENT BODY ODOR?

BAD BREATH

Good oral hygiene is especially important to avoid repelling others with smelly breath. Did you know that bad breath can be offensive not only to people but angels too?

> **Jabir bin Abdullaah narrated that the Messenger of Allaah ﷺ said: "He who eats of this (offensive) plant, garlic, (and sometimes he said: He who eats onion and garlic and leek) should not approach our masjid for the angels are offended by the same things as the children of Adam". - [Sahih Muslim]**

Smelly breath can come from not brushing, bad gum health, or a lack of saliva. Some people have a disease or infection that causes it, and we must treat them with kindness because it's not something they can control. However, for many of us, keeping our breath fresh is something we can manage, making a big difference in how people see us. So, how do we avoid this and keep our mouths clean and fresh?

A miswak is a twig that's been used as a toothbrush as far back as seven thousand years ago! Besides being a Sunnah for us Muslims, it's been used pre-Islaam by people in ancient China and Egypt, and to this day, in many parts of Africa and the Middle East.

A miswak contains many herbs and vitamins that fight tooth decay and cavities, prevent plaque, strengthen gums, and keep your breath fresh.

To use a miswak, peel off the hard outer shell to expose the smooth part underneath. Soak it in water for five minutes or so, chew on it to loosen the bristles and make them soft, and finally, in circular motions, rub the bristles over your teeth to clean them.

BAKING SODA

Brushing with Baking Soda not only gets rid of bad breath but also whitens your teeth. It prevents tooth decay and limits plaque buildup. It even remineralizes your enamel (the protective outer layer of your teeth).

To make your own baking soda toothpaste, you can simply mix a reasonable amount of baking soda with a little bit of water until it takes on a paste-like texture.

For a better tasting, and healthier toothpaste, mix 1 tsp of coconut oil, 1/2 a tsp of baking soda, 1/4 tsp of water, and 2-3 drops of peppermint or clove oil. Use as you would any other toothpaste.

TOOTHPASTE

Store-bought toothpaste is used to clean your teeth and prevent cavities. However, because of the harsh chemicals they're usually made of, it could be changing the chemistry of your saliva and causing more harm than good. The main ingredient in most toothpaste is fluoride. Try to avoid fluoride toothpaste, as it can be much too harsh on your mouth bacteria. This would be a good thing if it were only killing the bad ones, but too much can also kill the good bacteria that your mouth needs to keep your teeth and gums healthy and strong.

MOUTHWASH

Mouthwash is a quick and sure way to make your breath smell amazing, but isn't a replacement for actual brushing. Store bought mouthwash is usually made of harsh ingredients that destroy the balance of bacteria in your mouth, dry out the skin, may cause mouth ulcers, increase your risk for mouth cancer, and could even assist in making you develop gingivitis (a gum disease). Be sure to choose one made of natural ingredients to avoid these side effects.

FLOSSING

Flossing is key in caring for your teeth, as it removes food bits and other gunk that hides between each tooth. All sides of your teeth should be cleaned, not only what's seen on the outside. Always use a toothpick or floss strand after eating, and include this in your morning and evening brushing routine.

HOW AND WHEN TO BRUSH

Use a toothbrush with your preferred toothpaste. Dampen the bristles with water and brush in circular motions. Be sure to brush your tongue, and don't forget the back of your teeth. Do this for two minutes before rinsing your mouth with water. It is recommended to brush twice a day: once in the morning and once at night. **However, it's better to brush a few minutes after every meal.** This way, food doesn't settle on your teeth, preventing plaque and harmful bacteria from growing.

Remember, dear reader, things like gum and mints are not a replacement for brushing, or a solution for bad breath. It's only temporary and doesn't completely mask the bad smell. It also weakens your teeth, which causes bad breath more often and other health issues in the long run.

ARMPIT ODOR

One of the first signs of Puberty is when your armpits start to smell different. This is because sweat and bacteria gather under your arms, creating an odor. Bad eating habits or lack of hygiene can worsen armpit odor. Musty armpits can also ruin your reputation and make others not want to be around you. Here are a few ways to prevent this.

SHOWER

Depending on the season and how active you are throughout the day, you should shower everyday or at least three times a week. To prevent body odor, rinse the excess sweat, bacteria, and dirt buildup from your skin to give it a clean slate for the day. A shower routine will be given step by step in the later part of this chapter, Insha Allaah.

TAKE A BIRD BATH

Let's say you skipped a shower that day or can't take one for whatever reason. Instead, you can take a birdbath in the sink. Using soap and water lathered up in a washcloth, scrub your armpits to completely remove dirt buildup and bad odor. A washcloth is a hand towel that scrubs off all your dead skin cells without being harsh. When finished, be sure to clean the washcloth so your body odor doesn't transfer and build up on it.

USE DEODORANT

After showering or cleaning yourself, always use deodorant! If you don't, the odor will quickly come back to ruin your day. Never use deodorant without cleaning your armpits first. Using it on an unclean area won't fully mask the smell; if it does, you still have old chemicals, sweat, and bacteria built up on your skin.

However, always look at the deodorant ingredients and make sure there's no aluminum in them. Aluminum clogs your skin pores, preventing your body from sweating naturally, which is an important function for regulating temperature and keeping skin healthy. Aluminum has also been linked to certain health issues, like allergies and possibly breast cancer. For the same reasons, you should also avoid antiperspirants. Antiperspirants block your pores and prevent sweating. Your body needs to sweat to get rid of excess impurities, blocking them will only make them fester inside your skin, which can cause health problems.

DEODORANT WIPES

Deodorant wipes are a lifesaver! This is a must-have for every girl to keep in her purse. If you're at someone's house and don't want to use their shower or have been out all day and are starting to smell a little musty, you can grab a wipe and swipe until the smell is gone.

Please note, dear reader, that deodorant wipes and perfume are not a replacement for a shower or birdbath because they don't last all day. Perfume doesn't always mask the odor, making you smell both musty and flowery instead of clean. It also doesn't cleanse you and shouldn't be sprayed directly on sensitive armpit skin, as it can break you out and give you a rash.

Every girl has a natural vaginal scent that comes from discharge and healthy bacteria that live on your skin. **A healthy private area will have either no smell or a light sour, musky, and/or honeyed scent that is not overpowering or unpleasant.** During your menses, vaginal odor can become stronger since there's an added smell of blood. This doesn't mean it's unpleasant, but it does mean you must make more effort to keep yourself clean.

Being unhygienic, highly stressed, having unhealthy eating habits, or an infection can cause a pungent, salty, fishy, or foul scent in your private area. If you can catch an unpleasant whiff of yourself from 'down there' while casually sitting on the couch or doing daily activities, it's likely that others can, too. This is offensive to them and can be pretty embarrassing for you.

To prevent this, you must properly wash yourself after using the restroom and make healthier choices for your body. **In Islaam, we're taught to perform istinjaa—using water to cleanse the private area after relieving ourselves.** This is an obligatory act of cleanliness that can lead to torture in the grave if not followed!

> **Ibn Abbaas narrated that: "The Prophet ﷺ passed by two graves. He said, 'These two are being punished. And they are not being punished for something major. As for this one, he would not protect himself from his urine soiling his clothes. As for this one, he used to spread malicious gossip.'" - [at-Tirmidhi]**

Failing to cleanse yourself of urine and feces is not only unhealthy and stinky but also makes you spiritually impure. If you keep yourself spiritually impure, your prayers won't be valid. If your prayer is invalid because of your own purposeful actions, this is a great sin.

After properly cleaning themselves with water, most girls struggling with unpleasant vaginal odor will find that it completely goes away. To perform Istinjaa, there are many tools you can use. **A water sprayer** connects to your toilet and uses clean water from the tap. **A bidet** also uses clean water from the tap and connects to your toilet but precisely targets your private parts. **A portable bidet** is a must-have for every girl in her purse for the outside restroom since there's usually no other way to make istinjaa unless you bring a water bottle. This allows you to fill the small water container and squeeze it to target your area for cleaning. You can also use **a water can** to do the same.

All of the above are great ways to make istinjaa. After doing so, wipe with toilet paper or a clean washcloth to dry off or remove excess waste. Never wipe back to front, as the bacteria from your behind can get inside your vaginal area and cause an infection! **Always wipe front to back using your left hand, as is the Sunnah, then wash your hands with soap and water.**

> **Anas ibn Malik** said: "When the Prophet went out to relieve himself, another boy and myself would bring a vessel of water, meaning for him to clean himself with it." - [al-Bukhaari]

> **Aisha** said: "The right hand of the Messenger of Allaah was for his wudhoo and food, and his left hand was for cleaning himself after relieving himself and removing any filth." - [Abu Dawood]

Hygiene isn't the only thing that contributes to vaginal odor. What you wear can affect it, too.

Underwear that's too tight or made of rough fabric will irritate your private area. In fact, some fabrics even trap bacteria, sweat, and discharge, causing an unpleasant smell. This is why cotton is best for underwear—it's soft and gentle against your skin and allows your private area to breathe.

Never wear wet underwear, as it will trap bacteria, causing an unpleasant odor, irritation, rashes, and sometimes an infection. Always change your underwear every day to prevent rubbing against old bacteria and daily discharge.

Finally, what you put inside your body also affects vaginal odor. **Drink lots of water** to balance your hormones, and keep your vaginal canal lubricated and clean. **Cranberry juice** helps prevent infections and ease menstrual cramps; it also helps your immune system stay strong. **Eating pineapple** prevents infections and keeps your private area clean with a sweet scent. Lastly, **fruits of any kind** help cleanse the body, making you smell nice and fresh.

CLEANLINESS IN ISLAAM

Besides the istinjaa, there are other actions of cleanliness you must uphold as a Mukallaf Muslimah. All are obligatory and important for your health and worship.

WUDHOO

A Muslim is obligated to pray five times a day. Before praying, you must be physically and spiritually cleansed by offering wudhoo, or else your prayer won't be valid.

> **Abu Huraira narrated that the Messenger of Allaah ﷺ said: "The prayer of a person who does not perform wudhoo is not valid, and the wudhoo of a person who does not mention the name of Allaah (in the beginning) is not valid." - [Abu Dawood]**

HOW DO I OFFER WUDHOO?

1. SAY BISMILLAAH - Start by making the intention to offer wudhoo for the sake of worshiping Allaah. Then, begin in the name of Allaah.

2. WASH HANDS - Starting with your right hand first, wash your hands from the fingertips to your wrists.

3. RINSE MOUTH - Take some water into your mouth, swish it around to clean it, then spit it out.

4. CLEAN NOSE - With your right hand, sniff a reasonable amount of water up your nostrils; with your left, squeeze the excess water out.

5. WASH FACE - Scoop a reasonable amount of water into cupped hands and wash your face.

6. WASH ARMS - Starting with your right arm, wash from your fingertips to your elbows.

7. WIPE OVER YOUR HEAD - With the leftover water on your hands from washing your arms, wipe over the top of your head, from your hairline to the start of your neck.

8. CLEAN EARS - Use your index fingers and thumbs to gently clean the inside and outside of your ears, including behind them.

9. WASH FEET - Right foot first, wash your feet, being sure to get in between your toes to properly clean them.

Besides the head and ears (which should only be done once), do each step between 1-3 times, making sure to completely wash each area without leaving any dry spots; otherwise, you'll have to offer wudhoo again.

> **Umar bin Khattaab narrated that: "The Messenger of Allaah ﷺ saw a man performing wudhoo and he missed a spot the size of a fingernail on his foot. He commanded him to repeat the wudhoo and his prayer, so he did." - [Ibn Maajah]**

WHAT BREAKS MY WUDHOO?

- ✦ Urinating
- ✦ Defecating
- ✦ Passing gas
- ✦ Menstrual and postpartum bleeding
- ✦ Romantic intercourse
- ✦ Becoming unconscious
- ✦ Throwing up
- ✦ Sleeping

As long as you haven't done anything to break it, you can use the same wudhoo for multiple prayers.

> **Anas bin Malik narrated that: "The Messenger of Allaah ﷺ used to perform wudhoo for every prayer, and we used to perform all of the prayers with one wudhoo." - [Ibn Maajah]**

THE TEN ACTS OF THE FITRA

> **Aisha narrated that the Messenger of Allaah ﷺ said: "Ten are the acts according to fitra: clipping the mustache, letting the beard grow, using the tooth-stick, snuffing water in the nose, cutting the nails, washing the finger joints, plucking the hair under the armpits, shaving the pubes and cleaning one's private parts with water." The narrator said: "I have forgotten the tenth, but it may have been rinsing the mouth." - [Sahih Muslim]**

From this Hadeeth, we learn the ten acts of cleanliness that are natural to human beings (a part of our Fitra), and obligatory for each Muslim to do. They are:

1. Clipping the mustache (for men)
2. Letting the beard grow (for men)
3. Using a miswak
4. Cutting your nails
5. Plucking armpit hairs
6. Shaving pubic hair
7. Doing istinjaa
8. Keeping your hands and fingers clean
9. Rinsing your mouth (which is done during wudhoo)
10. Rinsing your nose (which is done during wudhoo)

The longest you can go without shaving, clipping your nails, and trimming the mustache (for men) is forty days. However, it's usually done more often than that.

> **Anas bin Malik narrated that: "The Messenger of Allaah ﷺ fixed forty days to shave the pubes, paring the nails, clipping the mustaches, and plucking the hair under the armpit." - [Abu Dawood]**

THE GHUSL

A ghusl is a full-body bath done to spiritually and physically cleanse yourself after specific impure actions. As a woman, you must take a ghusl when your menses are over and after releasing the type of discharge called maniy.

HOW DO I TAKE A GHUSL?

There are three methods you can choose from to properly take a ghusl.

Method one:

1. Say Bismillaah
2. Wash hands
3. Wash private parts
4. Offer wudhoo, but when you get to your head, fully submerge it in water so your scalp is thoroughly washed
5. Wash entire body from the neck down
6. Wash feet

Method two:

1. Say Bismillaah
2. Wash hands

3. Wash private parts

4. Offer wudhoo, but when you get to the arms, wash entire right side from the neck down, then do the same on the left

5. When you get to your head, fully submerge it in water so your scalp is thoroughly washed

6. Wash feet

When it comes to washing your head, If you have long hair, you don't have to wet all of it. The point is to get your scalp completely wet, not your hair.

In both of these methods, when it's time to wash your feet, you can either do it during wudhoo or wait until the end of the ghusl to do so.

Ibn Abbaas said: "My aunt Maymoonah told me, 'I brought the Messenger of Allaah water to do ghusl... ...He washed his hands two or three times, then he put his hand in the vessel and poured some water over his private part and washed it with his left hand. Then he struck his left hand on the ground and rubbed it vigorously (to clean them). Then he did wudhoo as one would do before praying, then he poured three handfuls of water over his head, then he washed the rest of his body. Then he moved away from the spot where he had been standing and washed his feet.'" - [al-Bukhaari]

Method three:

1. Say Bismillaah

2. Wash hands

3. Wash private parts

4. With the intention of making a ghusl, fully submerge your entire body in a clean body of water (like a bathtub, river, lake, etc). You must be covered in water all at once, not little by little.

Remember to do the ghusl only with your hands and water—no washing tool, soap, shampoo, or conditioner. If you're taking a shower that includes a ghusl, do that first, then your regular shower routine afterward.

The same things that break your wudhoo will break your ghusl. If you haven't done anything to invalidate it, you can pray after taking a ghusl without offering wudhoo.

A STEP BY STEP SHOWER ROUTINE

FULL SHOWER:

1. WASH YOUR HAIR
2. SCRUB YOUR BODY
3. RINSE
4. SHAVE
5. APPLY DEODORANT
6. MOISTURIZE
7. PERFUME

QUICK SHOWER:

1. SCRUB YOUR BODY
2. RINSE
3. APPLY DEODORANT
4. MOISTURIZE

WASH YOUR HAIR - Your hair-washing routine will depend on your hair type, which we'll learn about in a later chapter, Insha Allaah. Just know that if you're taking a shower that includes washing your hair, start with that first. This ensures that the shampoo and conditioner are thoroughly rinsed off your skin to prevent breakouts. It also lets you remove hair strands that might stick to your skin during the wash.

SCRUB YOUR BODY - On days you don't need to wash your hair, this is where you'll start, Insha Allaah. First, rinse your body with water, then choose your preferred washing tool. Next, choose a body wash or soap. Place your choice of soap on your cleaning tool and lather it up until it's nice and sudsy. Then, scrub your whole body. Neck, arms, armpits, chest, stomach, back, behind, and outer private area. Remember to keep soap of any kind away from the inside of your private area, or else it will sting and burn, and you can get an infection. Then, scrub your thighs, knees, calves, and feet. If the suds disappear, add more soap, lather, and keep going. To finish, rinse off all soap from your body with water.

SHAVE - If you're taking a shower and would like to shave, now is the time to do it. With your body free of dirt and dead skin, you're less likely to get ingrown hairs, and your shaving process will go much smoother. A full shaving routine will be explained in the next chapter, Insha Allaah.

MOISTURIZE - After shaving, or if you didn't need to, you can leave the shower. Use a towel to pat yourself dry, but not all the way. While your body is damp, apply a lotion, oil, or body butter of your choice to moisturize. Moisturizing is super important after showering because you've just scrubbed away your body's natural oils. You must restore the moisture that's been lost, especially in cold climates, when skin quickly becomes dry, chapped, or ashy. Make sure to moisturize every part of your body, including your face, neck, arms, chest, stomach, back, behind, legs, and feet.

DEODORANT - Next, wear deodorant, or your armpits will start smelling later. Keep in mind what was discussed before, and always choose an aluminum-free option.

PERFUME - If you aren't leaving the house after this shower (since it's Haraam to wear perfume outside) now's the time to apply perfume. Choose your favorite scent, preferably one that matches or complements the scent of your body soap and moisturizer.

After getting dressed, spray your clothes with the same perfume. Remember to always put on clean clothes after your shower. Never wear the same old, smelly clothing you wore before cleaning yourself.

WASHING TOOLS

A washcloth removes dead skin and dirt without being too harsh for everyday use. **A Loofah** doesn't scrub as well, but is gentle and gets the job done. Because of its shape, it easily traps bacteria and should be replaced every three to four weeks. **An African bath sponge** is gentle but coarse enough to remove dead skin and dirt. Its shape makes it easy to wash your back and other hard-to-reach places. **Exfoliating gloves or an exfoliating cloth** are great for a deep scrub but can be too harsh for everyday use. They can strip your body of its natural moisture, so it's better to use them only once a week.

You should never scrub your face with any washing tools listed above unless it's a washcloth. Everything else is too rough for your face since your facial skin is much more sensitive than your body's, and using these tools on your face can cause irritation, breakouts, or a rash. If you'd like, wash your face with water and do a simple skincare routine after the shower.

LAYERING SCENTS

If you want a stronger, sweeter scent, your soap or body wash should match the smell of your lotion, deodorant, and perfume. This is called layering scents. For example, If you have a vanilla body wash, you should also use vanilla lotion and perfume.

AVOIDING BACNE

It's better to use natural soaps to scrub your body since they usually have a strong, longer-lasting scent that will match nicely with most lotions and perfumes. Additionally, using natural soaps will help you avoid bacne (back acne), which sometimes happens when your skin reacts to harsh ingredients in chemically made body soaps.

WHAT SHOULD I USE TO MOISTURIZE?

Natural moisturizers like shea, mango, and cocoa butter or coconut, olive, and almond oil are best. These will nourish your skin deeper than most lotions, give you an earthy, clean smell, and keep your skin feeling soft and looking smooth and healthy, Insha Allaah.

PERFUME TIPS

The best places to apply perfume for a long-lasting scent are:

+ Behind your ears
+ Your neck
+ Under your chest
+ Wrists
+ Between your elbows
+ Behind your knees
+ Ankles

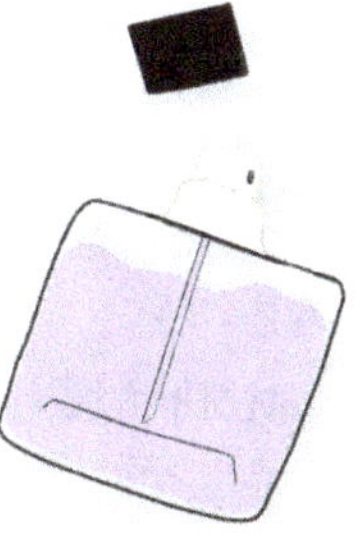

If your perfume scent doesn't last long enough, with the permission of an adult, melt some Vaseline and pour perfume into the liquid. Mix, and let harden in the fridge for a few hours. Vaseline is made to sit on top of your skin for many hours and lock in moisture; now, your new perfume mixture will do the same. Simply apply it to the same areas you normally would, and viola. **Do not spray perfume on sensitive areas like your face, armpits, or private area, this can break you out or cause a rash or infection.**

HOW TO SHAVE EVERYWHERE

Besides what's on your head, did you know that your body is covered in something called Vellus hair? These tiny wisps grow on your back, chest, stomach, and face. Their job is to protect you from micro bits of dirt and germs and help keep your body at a healthy temperature. As you grow, you'll start to see longer hair on your arms and legs; this is normal body hair and is there for the same reasons.

During Puberty, even fuller and thicker hair begins growing in your armpits and private area; this is pubic hair, and it protects your sensitive areas from skin irritation and infection.

Managing your new body hair may take some getting used to. Some girls are embarrassed by their hairy legs or arms and might especially feel self-conscious if others make fun of them for it.

Depending on how fast and thick the hair grows, it could be hard to keep up with constant shaving. Sometimes, the products and shaving tools you choose can give you dark spots, ingrown hairs, and little red bumps. It can be frustrating to have discolored skin underneath the hair or little nicks and irritation after a shave.

Body hair is nothing to be ashamed of. It's a natural development that everyone goes through and helps to keep your body safe. In fact, you should be proud that Allaah set your body up to care for itself this way. There's also a proper method for shaving to prevent and care for spots, bumps, and ingrown hairs, as well as to avoid nicking and cutting yourself by mistake.

HOW OFTEN SHOULD I SHAVE?

As Muslims, we must shave our pubic hair at least every forty days, as it is one of the ten acts of the Fitra. It is up to you if you'd like to shave more often than that.

If armpit hairs grow too long, deodorant, sweat, and bacteria can visibly build up into clumps within them. Similarly, longer pubic hairs can hold onto menstrual blood, discharge, sweat, urine, and feces, requiring more effort to clean.

Only you will know when your pubic hair gets to this point, but shaving once a week is enough, depending on how fast and thick your hair grows. If you are concerned about others seeing your armpit hair, shave it as frequently as you wish. However, if it doesn't bother you and isn't getting in the way of your cleanliness within the time our Prophet ﷺ set for us, you can let it be. You don't have to shave other body hair as that is not a requirement in Islaam, but if it's your preference or makes you feel uncomfortable, you can shave as you see fit.

SHAVING TOOLS

BODY RAZOR

A razor is the most common way to remove all types of body hair. You simply place conditioner or shaving cream over the spot you want to shave, then glide the razor over your skin, and it cuts the hair down.

Plastic disposable razors are the worst you can use, often leaving you with ingrown hairs, bumps, and dark spots. Razors with steel replaceable blades are reusable for much longer and cause less skin damage. Safety razors are best; they give the closest shave and are less likely to give you ingrown hairs and razor bumps.

FACIAL RAZOR

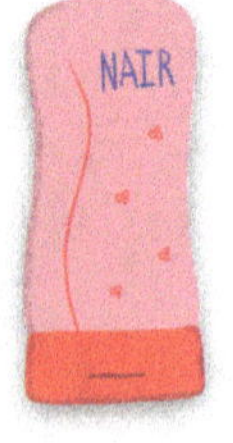

A facial razor is used for shaving eyebrow and vellus hair. In Islaam, it's Haraam to shape our eyebrows by shaving them. However, if you have a unibrow or visible mustache hairs, it's Halaal to get rid of it. Simply glide this over your skin, and the small hairs are shaved off.

NAIR

Nair is a chemical cream applied to your unwanted hair and left on for 4-10 minutes before wiping it off. Once cleared, the hair will have been removed. Many girls use this to protect themselves against ingrown hairs, but you can still get them if you don't prepare properly. Remember that Nair is a chemical that can burn your skin if you're sensitive or if it is left on too long. Always spot-test before using Nair, and follow the instructions on the packaging carefully.

BODY TRIMMER

A body hair trimmer is an electric trimmer that glides across your skin and the hair is cut. It is painless and safe, giving a clean cut for most areas of the body, while others are closely shaven.

WAXING

Waxing is done by melting waxing pearls, using kitchen ingredients to make sugar wax, or using sticky paper waxing strips. You place the wax on your skin as instructed on the packaging, let it harden slightly, then quickly pull it off to remove the hair from the root. This can be quite painful though, and you have to let your hair grow out a bit so the wax can catch it. Waxing is great for a clean, bare shave, and because the hair was pulled from the root, it takes a while to grow back. The more you do it, the less painful it becomes. Depending on how it's done, it can also prevent ingrown hairs.

EPILATOR

An epilator is a machine made of tiny tweezers. You glide it over your skin, and it pulls the hair from the root. Some say this is more painful than waxing; others say it's just as bad. Like waxing, it's great for a clean, bare shave and gets easier as you keep doing it. Because the hair is pulled from the root, it takes longer to grow back.

Laser hair removal is not for shaving but something you can use after you've done so. It's a laser that safely destroys your hair follicle so the hair will never grow back again. On lower levels, you won't feel anything, but if it's up to full power, you'll feel a zap that doesn't hurt but may surprise you. You have to use it every 3-4 days for 3-6 months before the hair completely stops growing, but in the meantime, you'll see the hair grow back slower and thinner, and it might be days, weeks, or even months before you have to shave again. When the hair is fully gone, you may need to get touch ups only every few years.

This device can be costly, but is well worth it if you can afford it and desire semipermanent removal of pubic, body, or facial hair.

HOW DO I REMOVE FACIAL HAIR?

Remember that you don't have to shave your face at all, but if you are uncomfortable with mustache or unibrow hairs, you're free to do so. You shouldn't shave the tiny vellus hairs on your forehead and cheeks, since they're unnoticeable most of the time, and if you shave them, things can easily get into your pores and break you out.

SHAVING:

1. CLEANSE
2. LUBRICATE
3. SHAVE
4. MOISTURIZE

NAIR:

1. CLEANSE
2. USE NAIR
3. CLEANSE AGAIN
4. MOISTURIZE

WAXING:

1. CLEANSE
2. WAX
3. MOISTURIZE

CLEANSE - Before shaving, clean your face with a natural soap or a cleanser. Avoid hand soaps and soaps with fragrance in them, as those can break you out. Any store-bought cleanser should work as long as it has no fragrance in it. Next, rinse your face with cold water since hot or warm water will open your pores, making it easy for you to break out and have rough-looking skin.

LUBRICATE - For a facial razor, use conditioner or shaving cream (you can also use soap if you don't have the other two) and place a reasonable amount over the area you want to shave. This will lubricate and soften the hair and skin so the razor blade can easily glide across; as well as help to prevent razor bumps, accidental nicks, and cuts. **Skip this step for Nair or waxing, as those methods require the skin to be clean and dry before use.**

✦ **FACIAL RAZOR -** For mustache or chin hair, use the face razor in the direction your hair grows, and not against it. Do it slowly to prevent razor bumps and to avoid shaving more than you intend to. For a unibrow, remember that you can shave the connecting hairs but not your actual brows since that is Haraam. This method causes the hair to grow back looking like stubble, which is fine if you plan to shave every few days. To avoid this, try waxing or Nair instead. Never use a regular body razor to shave your eyebrows since it's hard to control how much you take off with it.

✦ **WAXING -** Waxing the connecting unibrow hairs won't hurt as bad as waxing on your body, and only has to be done with one piece. The same applies to mustache hair. Heat up the wax, or use homemade sugar wax and lay it as instructed on the packaging or instructions you followed. Let it harden for a few seconds, then quickly rip it off in one go. You can also buy waxing strips specifically for a unibrow to make it easier.

✦ **NAIR** - A good way to get rid of mustache or unibrow hairs is Nair. Just be sure to use facial Nair only, and not the one made for the rest of your body. Body Nair is too strong for sensitive facial skin and can accidentally remove skin instead of only hairs. Place the cream over the hair you'd like to remove and thoroughly wash it off when the time is up. Make sure to closely follow the instructions on the packaging.

MOISTURIZE - After shaving, wash the area thoroughly and pat it dry until damp. Then, use a body oil, body butter, or moisturizer that doesn't have fragrance in it to hydrate the area. This is to prevent breakouts, irritation, and redness and to restore the natural oils you just scrubbed off.

HOW DO I REMOVE BODY AND PUBIC HAIR?

Your pubic areas are where you can easily get the most ingrown hairs, razor bumps, and dark spots. Be especially careful to follow these instructions to prevent them, and remember to shave within the time frame our Prophet ﷺ set for us. As for legs and arms, you don't have to shave them at all, but if you prefer it, follow these steps.

NAIR:

1. CLEANSE
2. USE NAIR
3. CLEANSE AGAIN
4. MOISTURIZE

SHAVING/TRIMMING:

1. CLEANSE
2. LUBRICATE
3. SHAVE/TRIM
4. ALCOHOL/TEND SKIN
5. MOISTURIZE

WAXING:

1. CLEANSE
2. WAX
3. MOISTURIZE

EXFOLIATE & CLEANSE - If you're shaving wet using a razor or trimmer, exfoliate and cleanse your pubic hairs by using a sugar scrub, which should be lathered into the desired area and rinsed off. If you can't use a sugar scrub, an exfoliating cloth should do the trick almost as well. This is to get rid of the dirt, bacteria, sweat, and dead skin so you can remove the hair on a clean surface. This is key to preventing ingrown hairs and razor bumps, as well as erasing old dark spots over time. For arms and legs, a washcloth or exfoliator glove will work just fine.

LUBRICATE - For a razor or trimmer, use conditioner or shaving cream (you can also use soap if you don't have the other two) and place a reasonable amount over the area you want to shave. This will lubricate and soften the hair and skin so the razor blade can easily glide across; as well as help to prevent razor bumps, accidental nicks, and cuts. **Skip this step for Nair or waxing, as those methods require the skin to be clean and dry before use.**

✦ **RAZOR** - Applying gentle pressure, carefully shave downward for armpit hair. Only a few short passes should be needed to get the job done. It's not necessary to shave upwards under your arms, as that will irritate your skin and cause ingrown hairs and bumps.

For arms and legs, shave in long strokes up or down (whichever direction you prefer). Only one or two passes on the same spot are required to do the job.

For the private area, if the pubic hair has grown a considerable amount, you may want to trim it short using a body trimmer or pair of scissors first. Otherwise, the razor may not be effective and could get jammed.

For private area pubes, start by slowly but firmly shaving downward (in the direction of the hair growth). If you need a closer shave, you can then shave side to side. If you choose to shave upwards for a completely bare shave, do so very carefully with plenty of lubrication so you don't cut yourself or irritate your sensitive skin. Shaving upward causes the most razor bumps and irritation.

Remember to use new disposable razors every time or only clean reusable ones. Avoid rushing—wait until you have enough time to shave carefully. You only need to make a few passes with the razor on each spot. Doing so slowly with gentle pressure will make your area look much smoother. As you shave, the razor will fill with hair, so you should rinse it every two to three swipes to prevent jamming and dullness. When you're done, rinse off the fallen hair with water.

✦ **TRIMMER** - Carefully run the trimmer across your skin in the same direction you use a razor. A body trimmer will give a bare shave for the arms and legs, but not pubic hair, which will be closely shaven instead. If you'd like a bare shave, use another method.

- ✦ **NAIR** - When choosing Nair, be sure to patch test first and then use it as instructed on the packaging. Place a medium layer of cream where you want to remove the hair, let it sit for 4-10 minutes depending on how thick the hair is, and rinse it off thoroughly with water.

Be especially careful not to place Nair inside the lips of your private area, or near the main hole. This can cause a terrible itching and burning sensation, and leave you with a painful infection.

- ✦ **WAXING -** If you'd like to wax, it's a good idea to watch a YouTube tutorial on how to do so depending on which wax you decide to use. But in general, heat the wax, lay it against the growth of the hair, let it harden for a few seconds, and then rip it off quickly. Especially on your pubic areas, waxing is painful, but gets easier after a few uses.

RUBBING ALCOHOL OR TEND SKIN SOLUTION - This step can be skipped for arm and leg hair. After you've finished shaving your pubic areas and rinsed the hair off with water, make sure to pat the spot completely dry. Take a few drops of rubbing alcohol on a cotton swab or piece of tissue, gently dab it onto the area you just shaved, and let it dry.

Rubbing alcohol is an antiseptic that gets rid of razor bumps and ingrown hairs while preventing infection, especially after shaving the pubic areas. The first few times you do this, it might sting because you're applying a drying chemical to a freshly shaven spot. But after a few uses it won't sting at all, Insha Allaah.

If you don't want to use pure rubbing alcohol, you can use another product called Tend Skin Solution. This should be applied after shaving the same way you would alcohol. Always be sure to spot test before using a new product, and feel free to find another aftershave if this one doesn't work for you.

You should use either of these options twice a day after shaving. If you still notice razor bumps, continue applying once a day until they disappear, which usually takes about 1-2 days.

Despite it being crucial after shaving, either one will dry your skin, which is why **you should never do this step without moisturizing.**

MOISTURIZE - After allowing the rubbing alcohol or Tend Skin Solution to set in and dry, it's time to moisturize. Use body oil, body butter, or a moisturizer like vaseline or a non-fragranced lotion to hydrate the area, which will make your skin soft and supple.

Moisturizing prevents breakouts, irritation, and redness and restores the natural oils that you just scrubbed, shaved, and dried off. For armpits, only apply a thin layer of moisture so that it doesn't block your deodorant from doing its job.

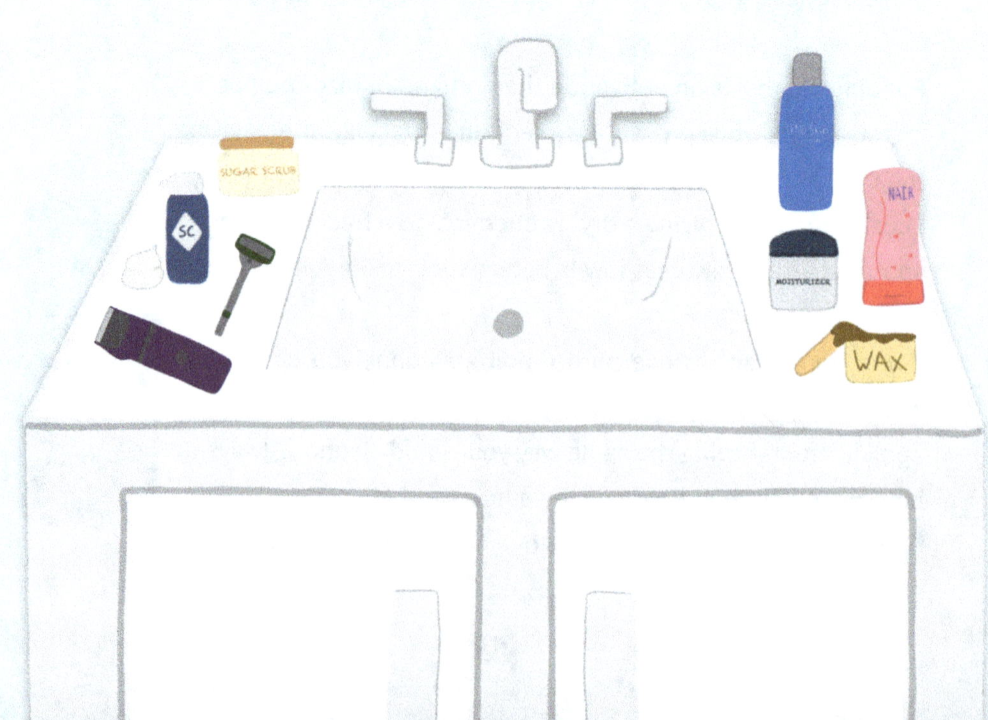

MENSTURAL CARE

Getting your menses (aka your period) is one of the signs that you are officially mukallaf. Once a month, drops of blood will flow from your private area for around 5-7 days. This may sound scary, but it's actually a normal and healthy process that shows your body is running as it should. Knowledge is power, and the more you learn about your period, the less daunting it will be, Insha Allaah.

WHY DO I GET MY MENSES?

It all starts from organs inside your body called the ovaries. Inside your ovaries are thousands of eggs. Each month, to prepare for reproduction (the process of having a baby), an egg journeys through the ovaries and the fallopian tube to reach your uterus. Your uterus is lined with extra blood and tissue to nourish and protect a baby in case you become pregnant. However, if there is no baby, your body gets rid of the extra blood and tissue by pushing it out through the vagina (your private area) over the course of a week or so, which is the bleeding you see during your menses. This monthly process is called a menstrual cycle.

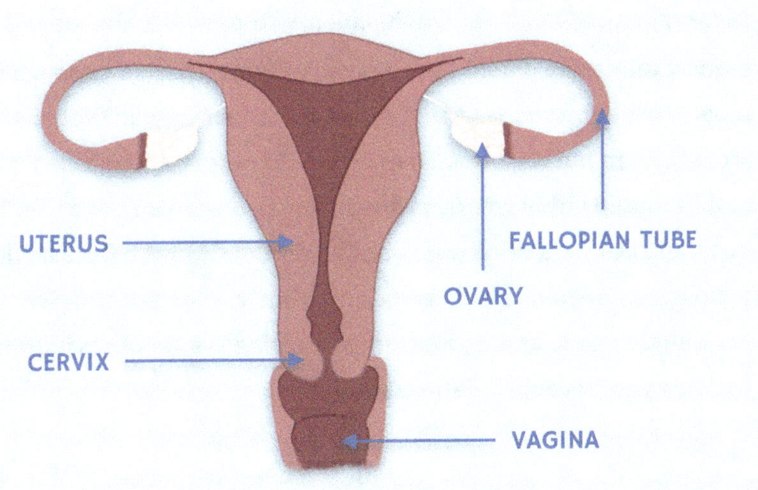

WHAT DOES ISLAAM SAY ABOUT MENSES?

Before the time of the Prophet ﷺ, and still in some cultures today, women were not allowed in certain spaces or to do things like eating, drinking, or spending time with family when they were menstruating. They were considered dirty, or less than, just because of their body's natural process.

Our Prophet Muhammad ﷺ did not follow this example and told his companions that there are no restrictions on how to act with their wives while on their menses except for romantic intercourse. There are many instances in Hadeeth where the wives of the Prophet ﷺ speak of times they spent with him during their menses, showing us to act normal and not let our menses get in the way of everyday life.

Aisha ﷺ narrated that: "The Prophet ﷺ used to embrace me during my menses. He also used to lean his head out of the masjid while he was in I`tikaaf, and I would wash it during my menses." - [al-Bukhaari]

Shuraih narrated that he asked Aisha ﷺ : "Can a woman eat with her husband while she is menstruating? She said: 'Yes. The Messenger of Allaah ﷺ would call me to eat with him while I was menstruating. He would take a piece of bone on which some bits of meat were left and insist that I take it first, so I would nibble a little from it, then put it down. Then he would take it and nibble from it, and he would put his mouth where mine had been on the bone. Then he would ask for a drink and insist that I take it first before he drank from it. So I would take it and drink from it, then put it down, then he would take it and drink from it, putting his mouth where mine had been on the cup.'" - [an-Nasaa'i]

> **Aisha ؓ narrated that: "The Prophet ﷺ used to lean on my lap and recite Quraan while I was on my menses." - [al-Bukhaari]**

It is a common misconception that you cannot hold a Mus'Haf while on your menses. Although this is widely practiced, with women wearing gloves or using an electronic device to read their portion for the day, there is no direct statement of this in the Quraan and Sunnah. In fact, there is a Hadeeth that suggests the opposite.

> **Aisha ؓ narrated that: "The Messenger of Allaah ﷺ said to me, 'Get me the prayer mat from the Masjid.' I replied, 'I am menstruating.' He said, 'Your menstruation is not in your hand.'" - [Sahih Muslim]**

If your parents or caretakers tell you not to touch the Quraan while on your menses, there is no harm in following their orders if they don't know or disagree with this. As long as you know it is not a sin for you and the rule has been enforced through culture instead of Islaam, that's what matters.

The actions that should be avoided during your menses have been made clear in the Quraan and Sunnah. Acts of worship that require wudhoo are not Halaal to do while you are on your menses, because the blood includes impurities that invalidate it. These acts of worship are praying, fasting, and making tawaf around the Ka'bah. Once your menstrual bleeding has stopped, you must take a ghusl before being able to do them again.

> **Aisha ؓ narrated that: "The Prophet ﷺ said to me, 'Give up the prayer when your menses begin and when it has finished, wash the blood off your body (take a ghusl) and start praying.'" - [al-Bukhaari]**

> Abu Sa`id Al-Khudri narrated that while the Prophet ﷺ was advising a group of women, he said: "Isn't it true that a woman can neither pray nor fast during her menses?" The women replied in the affirmative. He said, "This is the deficiency in her religion." - [al-Bukhaari]

> Aisha narrated that: "I was menstruating when I reached Mecca. So, I neither performed Tawaf of the Ka`ba, nor the Tawaf between Safa and Marwa. Then I informed Allaah's Messenger ﷺ about it. He replied, 'Perform all the rites of Hajj like the other pilgrims, but do not perform Tawaf of the Ka`bah till you have purified yourself (from your menses).'" - [al-Bukhaari]

WHEN WILL I GET MY MENSES?

Every girl is different and develops at her own pace. Even girls in the same family may get their first period at different ages. **You can get your first menses anytime between the ages of 8-15 (with the average age being 12)**, and although you might not know exactly when it will happen, there are signs that show you may be getting it soon.

Once you start developing other Puberty signs like discharge, growing breasts, and pubic hair, your menses will not be far off and can come anytime within the next year or so.

If you've already begun your menses but don't know when it will come every month, there are a set of symptoms you can get that indicate your period is likely a few days away. **This set of symptoms is called Premenstrual Syndrome, or PMS for short.**

Emotional PMS symptoms:

- Being tense or anxious
- Being extra depressed
- Crying spells
- Mood swings, irritability, and anger
- Food cravings
- Trouble falling asleep
- Withdrawing from friends and family
- Not being able to concentrate

Physical PMS symptoms:

- Joint or muscle pain
- Cramps
- Headaches
- Fatigue
- Weight gain
- Bloating in the abdomen
- Breast tenderness
- Acne breakouts
- Constipation or diarrhea

Remember, you won't experience all of these symptoms, and some girls don't have any. Most girls will notice a pattern of a few symptoms that usually show up a week or so before the menses begin and continue during it.

HOW LONG DOES THE BLEEDING LAST?

How long the menses lasts depends on the girl. For some, it only lasts three days, and for others, seven or eight. **For most girls, it lasts between 5-7 days.** In Islaam, the longest your period can last is 15 days; if you are still bleeding beyond this, it is considered irregular bleeding. This is not a good sign and should be checked by a doctor. Irregular bleeding is not counted as menses in Islaam, and you are required to pray, fast, and carry on as usual while on it, as said in this Hadeeth:

Aisha narrated that: "Umm Habibah bint Jahsh suffered Istihadah (irregular bleeding) for seven years. She complained about that to the Messenger of Allaah ﷺ and he said: 'That is not menstruation; rather that is (bleeding from) a vein, so perform ghusl then pray.' So she would perform ghusl for each prayer." - [at-Tirmidhi]

Your regular menses will come every month for the rest of your life unless you become pregnant, are very sick, or have reached a time called menopause, which is when you have passed the age of being able to have children. Menopause usually starts in a woman's early fifties.

HOW DO I PREPARE FOR MY MENSES?

TAKE CARE OF YOUR BODY

The key to a smooth period is to prepare for it before it starts. First, apply what you learned from the chapter on caring for your body inside. Eating well, staying active, and being clean, will keep your body healthy, which prevents period symptoms from becoming overwhelming or painful. It will also give you the tools needed for avoiding vaginal infections and keeping your private area from smelling bad and becoming irritated.

As soon as you notice you're having PMS symptoms, prepare for your menses by drinking lots of water and cranberry juice. This will be very helpful for relieving cramps, acne breakouts, and headaches.

HAVE THE NEEDED SUPPLIES

Because you may not know when your period is coming, every girl should have the following items both at home and in their purse for when they need them. This isn't just for those who already have their period; if you are showing other signs of Puberty and think you might get it within that year, you should be equally prepared.

MUST HAVES AT HOME:

✦ Pads (or your other choice of period products)
✦ A clean set of underwear (black is best since the color hides blood stains)
✦ A wet bag (to store messy underwear until you wash them)

- ✦ A heating pad or blanket for cramps, back pain, or muscle aches
- ✦ Over-the-counter pain relievers for cramps, back pain, or muscle aches

MUST HAVES IN YOUR PURSE:

- ✦ Two pads (or your other choice of period products)
- ✦ A spare pair of underwear (black is best since the color hides blood stains)
- ✦ A big ziplock, small plastic bag, or a wet bag for messy underwear
- ✦ An over-the-counter pain reliever like Ibuprofen, Tylenol, or Motrin
- ✦ A portable Bidet or water bottle for istinjaa on the go

TRACK YOUR CYCLE

When you first start getting your menses, it's a good idea to keep track of it. The first few periods may not come at the same time each month. It takes a little while for your body to adjust and for your menses to come in a noticeable pattern.

This is why you should use period tracking apps or a regular calendar to track your menses. You can note down when your menses come, how heavy or light your flow was, your feelings, and your symptoms. This will make it easy for you to spot when your period starts a pattern and can help you estimate when the next one is coming.

It's also great for tracking your mood; even if you don't notice it, anger, depression, or anxiousness can also come in a pattern during Puberty.

KNOW HOW TO PUT TOGETHER A MAKESHIFT PAD

Suppose you've forgotten your purse, and your period starts unexpectedly when you're not at home. You'll have to ask someone for a pad, or rush to the store to get one, but what do you do in the meantime? Here are two ways to make a pad with things you'll probably have on the go, or even at home if you ran out of period products, Insha Allaah.

I. WRAP TOILET PAPER AROUND UNDERWEAR

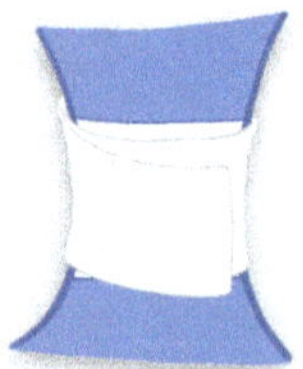

Get to a bathroom, clean yourself up, and wrap toilet paper around the middle part of your underwear about 5-10 times. It won't last long and can leak fast, so you must be quick to find a new pad, or you'll have to change it very often.

2. FOLD A SOCK AND WRAP TOILET PAPER AROUND UNDERWEAR

This method is almost the same as the first, except you fold a sock in half so it fits in the middle part of your underwear and wrap the tissue around 5-10 times to secure it. This will last longer than the first method and won't leak as easily, either.

WHAT IS MENSTRUAL BLOOD LIKE?

You'll know you have your menses when you feel a wetness in your underwear that is a bit uncomfortable and sometimes sticky. When you look, you'll find blood that is thicker than the usual blood from a cut, for example. Menstrual blood smells like regular blood, but slightly more metallic and mixed with your normal vaginal scent. At the beginning or end of your menses, it could be a burgundy or dark brown color, but is usually red. Sometimes a blood clot can come out with your flow, which looks like a tiny piece of bloodied jelly flesh. This is normal, but might hurt or feel strange coming out.

MENSTRUAL DISCHARGE COLORS

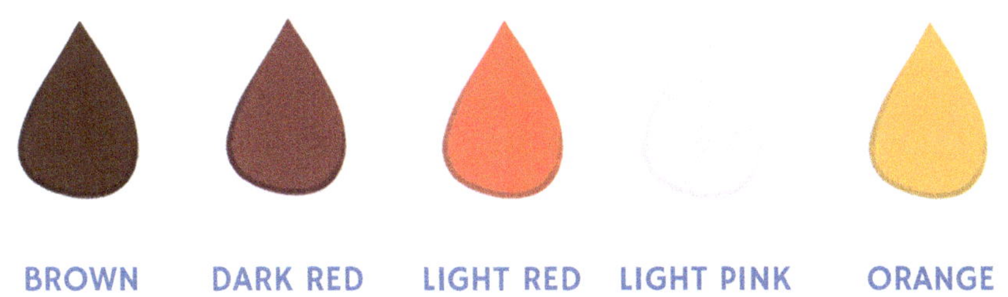

| BROWN | DARK RED | LIGHT RED | LIGHT PINK | ORANGE |

Brown is oxidized (mixed with oxygen) older blood that can show up at the beginning or end of your period.

Dark red is oxidized blood that can show up at the beginning or end of your period.

Light red is fresh blood that flows on regular and heavier days of your menses.

Light pink is menses blood mixed with vaginal discharge.

Orange is menses blood mixed with vaginal discharge, can also be a sign of infection if it happens outside your period.

MENSTRUAL PRODUCT OPTIONS

DISPOSABLE SANITARY PADS

A disposable sanitary pad is something that sticks inside your underwear, and the wings adhere around the bottom outside so it doesn't move around. They must be changed every 3-4 hours, and some are made without wings for those who prefer it. You shouldn't use just any pad that you find at the store, since most are made with chlorine bleach to give it an extra clean, white appearance.

This toxic chemical being exposed to your private area over time can cause issues like hormone dysfunction, asthma, pelvic inflammatory disease, fertility impairment, and cancer. May Allaah protect us all from that, Ameen.

Thankfully in this case, healthier doesn't mean more expensive, and brands such as L. and The Honey Pot Company offer non-bleached, one hundred percent cotton disposable pads for an affordable price. Feel free to find other brands that suit your menstrual needs if these don't work for you.

CLOTH PADS

Cloth pads are great if you want to avoid chemicals altogether. The wings on these snap in place, and the material is usually made of soft cotton, which is much better for your sensitive areas.

The outer layer is leak proof, and you change them every 3-4 hours like disposable pads. They must be washed after use, and when they wear out after a few years, you replace them. Although cloth pads are made slim, they feel bulkier than most disposable pads and can be uncomfortable to be active in. You can also get these in different sizes to meet the needs of your period flow.

TAMPONS

A tampon is a cotton piece with string attached that goes up your private area and absorbs blood from the inside. Although most people choose this for comfort, it can be unhealthy compared to other methods, and a bit difficult to properly use at first.

Because tampons absorb any liquid and not just blood, it blocks your natural discharge from coming out, causing all the bad bacteria to stay inside your private area; the over-absorption can also dry out your vaginal canal. Tampons put you at a higher risk of infection and often have the same chloral bleaching as sanitary pads. However, just like pads you can find tampons made without unhealthy materials for an affordable price.

There is a difference of opinion in Islaam as to whether or not tampons are Halaal to use. Ask your mom what opinion she follows, and go according to that. Never stop learning about Islaam, so that you can make your own informed decision one day.

DISPOSABLE PERIOD UNDERWEAR

Disposable period underwear are a good choice for girls who have a heavy flow and might leak through other options, especially at night. They're very comfortable to wear, but sometimes make noise when you're moving about, and could be made from the same harmful materials in some disposable pads.

PERIOD UNDERWEAR

Period underwear are just like normal underwear but has special absorbent material to prevent leaks during your period. They are great for girls who want to feel like they aren't even on their menses. Just remember that you have to wash them after use, and if you don't get the right ones, you can feel the blood sitting on top instead of being absorbed, which is very uncomfortable.

The good ones are usually not cheap and you have to change them at least three times a day. Having at least four pairs is wise, meaning you'll likely need to wash them daily rather than waiting until the end of your cycle to do so.

You can also use these underwear along with a pad for extra protection if you're afraid of leaking; or on their own at the end of your period when you don't need a full pad, but aren't sure if you're completely done bleeding.

PAD ABSORBENCY LEVELS

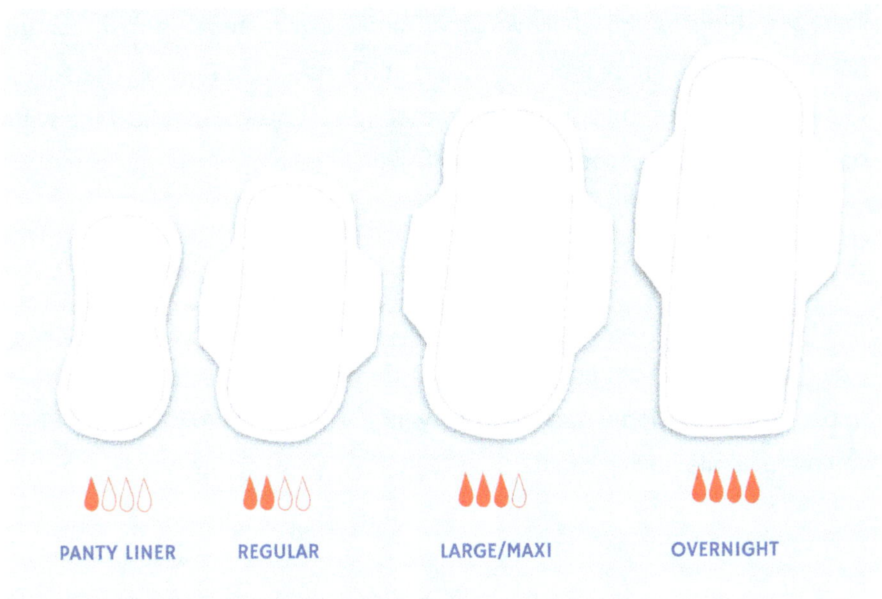

Panty liners are very small and thin pads for light drops of blood at the end of menses. Some people wear panty liners outside of their menses to catch discharge or when they think their period is coming, but don't want to waste a full pad until it's really there.

Regular pads are made bigger than liners but still thin for comfort. They hold a lot more blood and are a good choice for most or all of your menses unless your flow is heavier that day.

Large pads are made larger and thicker than regular pads for heavy flow. They are a good choice if you experience a lot of blood flow during the first few days of your period or on days when you're very active and need extra absorbency.

Overnight pads are the longest and largest of the rest so you don't have to worry about leaks while you sleep. You can also wear them during the day if needed.

HOW AND WHEN TO CHANGE A PAD

The first thing to do when you feel blood 'down there' is rush to the bathroom with a change of underwear and a new pad. Take off the soiled underwear and wash yourself with water, (do Istinjaa). Dry and wipe with tissue or a washcloth (front to back).

USING A PAD

To use a pad, take it out of the package, peal the seals off, lay the sticky side down on your underwear, and fold the wings behind to adhere them to the underside. Some pads have no wings, and that's okay. Choose what you prefer while buying them.

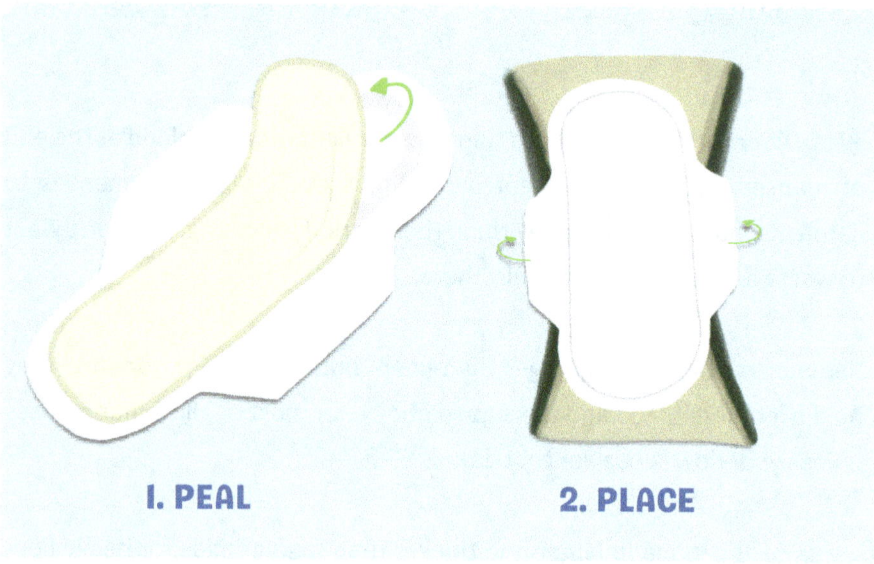

WHEN TO CHANGE IT

You have to change your pad every 3-4 hours and each time you use the restroom. Not just because your pad will be full but also to clean yourself and prevent an odor. Period blood has a light metallic scent, if you let the blood build up for too long, it will take on a heavy, musty smell and later begin to stink.

WHAT TO DO WITH THE OLD ONE

To get rid of the used pad, fold it in half twice, with the blood on the inside, or roll it into a tube. Then wrap it in toilet paper so it's fully covered, and place it in the trash. **Never flush a pad down the toilet.**

This is so that others coming behind you won't see your pad full of blood and also to keep the smell from spreading around the bathroom. After this, thoroughly wash your hands with soap and water.

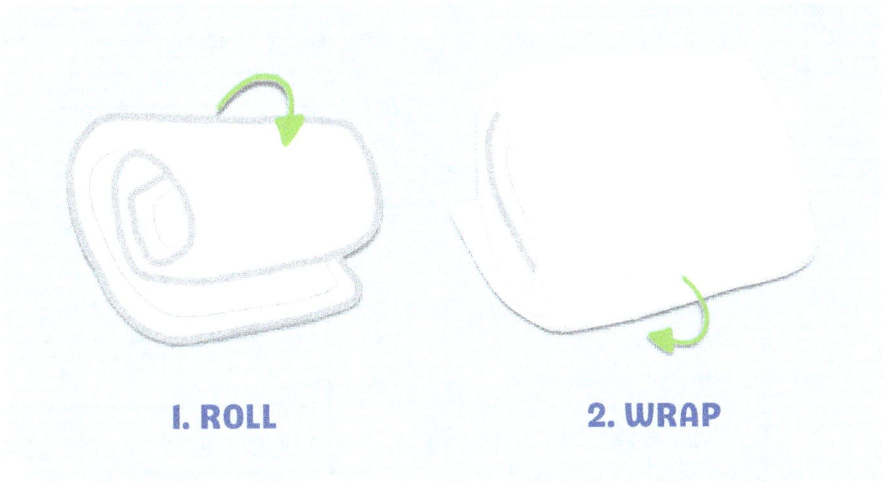

HOW DO I CARE FOR MENSTRUAL SYMPTOMS?

Physical Symptoms:

+ Joint or muscle pain
+ Cramps
+ Lower back pain
+ Headaches
+ Fatigue

- ✦ Weight gain
- ✦ Bloating in the abdomen
- ✦ Breast tenderness
- ✦ Acne breakouts
- ✦ Food Cravings
- ✦ Constipation or diarrhea

HOW TO MANAGE PHYSICAL PMS SYMPTOMS:

- Drink lots of water and cranberry juice before and during your menses

- Drink lots of tea, chamomile, fennel, and ginger tea are great for cramps

- Take an over the counter pain reliever like Ibuprofen, Motren, Tylenol, etc, for cramps, backpain, or headaches. (Ask an adult which one is best)

- Take a hot bath for cramps and back pain

- Stay active and do some light exercises

- Use heating pads where your cramps are

- Sleep whenever you can

- Give in to your cravings! (As long as it doesn't make you sick!)

Emotional Symptoms:

- ✦ Being tense or anxious
- ✦ Being extra depressed
- ✦ Crying spells
- ✦ Mood swings, irritability, and anger
- ✦ Trouble falling asleep

✦ Withdrawing from friends and family

✦ Not being able to concentrate

HOW TO MANAGE EMOTIONAL PMS SYMPTOMS:

• Say your morning and evening athkaar, especially since you aren't praying

(can be found in the free Husnul Muslim app or book)

• Say the Duaa's against anxiety, depression, sadness, and anger (can also

be found in the free Husnul Muslim app or book)

• Don't take anger or irritation out on people who don't deserve it, if you

know your real feelings are stemming from menstrual discomfort, not them

• Still read Quraan, but with the intention of putting peace in your heart

• Try to recognise when the intense feelings are from the situation, v.s.

your menstrual symptoms, and react accordingly

• Read the chapter: Dealing with Feelings (Starting on page 107)

HOW DO I KNOW MY MENSES IS OVER?

As a Muslim, knowing when your menses is over is very important because you have to start praying again. During the last day or so of your period, the blood will drip out very slowly and very little. Sometimes, hours will go by with nothing in your pad, but just when you're about to take a ghusl, you might notice a spot.

Because the color of menstrual blood can change towards the end of your period to light brown, orange, or pink, it can be difficult for some girls to know when they are fully clear of their menses.

You are officially off your menses when there is no blood at all and your discharge runs white or clear.

A great way to know when the blood has stopped is by using a Kursuf. This was used in the Prophet's ﷺ time by the women around him. A Kursuf is a small, white, square, or rectangular cloth that is folded in half and placed between the lips of your vagina opening on the last day of your menses. You can also use a cotton ball or a square of tissue.

Put on your underwear and go about your day as usual. At every prayer, pull it out and check if there is anything on it. If there is, use a new cloth, swab, or piece of tissue to do it again. This will show you when you are done bleeding quicker than waiting to see if your pad is clean because the blood doesn't have to drip all the way down for you to see it.

If the Kursuf comes out either dry or with white or clear discharge after 5-6 hours since your last lightly colored spotting, you're ready to pray and can take a ghusl.

> It was narrated that Umm 'Alqamah said: "The women used to send to Aisha the Mother of the Believers vessels in which were their rags, on which there was yellowish discharge from menstrual bleeding, asking her about prayer, and she would tell them 'Do not hasten until you see the white discharge'." - [al-Bukhaari]

DOES THE GHUSL CHANGE FOR MENSES?

The way you take a ghusl does not change for your menses; follow the same instructions as shown in the chapter of Keeping Clean and Smelling Good. If you are wearing a style where your hair is braided closely to your head, you can keep them in as long as the water can reach your scalp.

WHAT SHOULD I DO AFTER A GHUSL?

After the ghusl, you are ready to pray and do not have to do anything else. However, it is the Sunnah to purify your private area with black musk. Just make sure that it is pure black musk and not mixed with chemicals or anything to dilute or stretch it, as these could lead to infections. Pure black musk helps to prevent vaginal infections, naturally perfumes your private area, and cleans it of impurities.

Simply take a cotton swab and add one drop of musk to it (a little goes a very long way). Wipe around the lips of your private area, and at the entrance of where the blood comes out.

During your menses it's normal to feel little down, sluggish, and some discomfort from cramps or other period symptoms. But in general, your life should be able to go on as normal without your period getting in the way of daily activity and having fun.

Although every girl is different, your menses should never be a time of overwhelming pain or discomfort. If you're dreading your monthly visitor because of any reason on the list below, it's definitely time to get checked by a doctor.

- If your period lasts more than seven days
- If you constantly have irregular bleeding
- If you experience severe cramping, back pain, diarrhea, and/or headaches
- If the time between each menses is two months or more instead of one
- Constantly passing blood clots that are the size of a quarter or bigger
- Having such heavy flow that you have to change your period product every hour or less

Part Two

ISLAAM & EMOTIONS

OBLIGATIONS AND SPIRITUAL NEEDS

Have you ever woken up feeling odd without knowing why? You go through the day the same way you always do: take a shower, eat breakfast, brush your teeth, get ready for the day, go to school, do some chores, play a bit, eat some more, get ready for bed, and then snuggle under your covers. The day was normal. You can't think of anything unusual that happened. Yet, as you lie in bed, you feel different inside.

You're uninterested. Nothing excites you, and you aren't particularly looking forward to tomorrow. The days are becoming a drag and blending together in your memory. There's a hint of sadness or longing deep inside you. You're waiting for things to get better, for things to be fun again. Right now, everything has become meaningless and empty, and your heart is beginning to feel less and less alive.

This, dear reader, is a sign that your soul needs some care.

Now that you are going through Puberty and your body and mind are changing, you will find that your spiritual needs will begin to grow, and it is important that you pay attention to them. It's not enough to only care for physical changes, you need to take care of who you are inside. You have to look within, or else the state of your heart and mind can overtake you and turn you into a person you didn't want to become.

If you're feeling particularly empty, sad, or moody for no clear reason, or if you have been doing your best to get rid of those feelings and they just won't go away, this is a sign that your spiritual needs are not being met.

Just like your mind and body, your soul needs care too. If your soul is not at peace, your heart and mind won't be either, and your body will feel the effects. Just because you can't see your soul doesn't mean you can ignore it. Where do you think your emotions, desires, and gut feelings come from? You can't see those either, but you know they're there and affect your daily life.

If you live your life ignoring your spiritual needs, you'll find that depression, anxiety, bad decisions, and sinful deeds can come in a constant and hopeless cycle that feels like it'll never end.

Now that you are Mukallaf, dear reader, it is obligatory for you to follow Allaah's commands and stay away from what He has forbidden, as you'll learn, this is not without reason.

Because He created us, Allaah knows our souls need care, which is why He gave us the religion of Islaam. If we follow the way of life He designed for us, our souls will be properly cared for, and our lives will become fulfilling, productive, and meaningful as a result.

WHAT IS THE SOUL?

"And indeed We created man out of an extract of clay. Thereafter We placed him as a drop of fluid in a safe place. Then We made the drop of fluid into a clinging clot, then We made the clot into a little lump of flesh, then We made out of that little lump of flesh bones, then We clothed the bones with flesh... "- [Quraan, 23:12-14]

In suratul-Mu'minoon, Allaah explains the process of human creation. At this point where the ayah has been cut off, it is describing the first two months in the mother's womb. However, the baby is not yet alive, and is simply a growing body without life.

In this Hadeeth, our Prophet ﷺ is telling us about when Allaah created the body of Prophet Adam, and Shaytaan began to observe him. Notice when Prophet Adam's body was created but didn't have a soul, it is referred to as a 'hollow" body, meaning there was no life within it.

The ayah about our creation on the previous page (23:14) ends with: **"...and then We bought it forth as another creation."** meaning that Allaah gave the body a soul, making it into a new creature, a living human being that can see, hear, understand, and move around. This is further backed up by the following ayaat.

In Suratul-Hijr, where Allaah tells us how He created Prophet Adam's body and told the angels to prostrate to him; we learn that Allaah breathed into Adam the soul that He created for him.

> **Abu Hurairah** ﷺ **narrated that the Messenger of Allaah** ﷺ **said: "When Allaah created Adam, He breathed the soul into him, then he sneezed and said: 'All praise is due to Allaah.' So he praised Allaah by His permission. Then His Lord said to him: 'May Allaah have mercy upon you, Oh Adam...'" - [at-Tirmidhi]**

In this Hadeeth, we learn that when Allaah breathed the soul into Adam, as it came into him from the top of his head down, he sneezed when it reached his nose, and said AlHamdulillaah when it came to his mouth, and so on.

It is the soul Allaah has given you that brings your body to life. Without the soul, your body is simply flesh. The soul is the essence of who you are, and that is why even if horrible things happen to the body, leaving it not working in some way (may Allaah protect us from that, Ameen), people still live in some cases because it is only when Allaah takes the soul from the body that we actually die.

Now that you know what a soul is, you must learn how to take care of it. Just like how Allaah gave you a body to use and take care of, He gave you a soul to do the same and fulfill your purpose in this life.

> **"Oh you who believe! Take care of your souls. If you follow the right guidance, no hurt can come to you from those who are in error..." - [Quraan 5:105]**

WHAT ARE YOUR SPIRITUAL NEEDS?

Spiritual is the word used when talking about the soul or spirit, which means the same thing in this case. Spiritual needs are the mindset and actions your soul requires to stay pure, healthy, and strong.

SPIRITUAL NEEDS:

- TO KNOW THE MEANING OF LIFE
- TO KNOW WHO ALLAAH IS
- TO DO THE OBLIGATORY ACTS OF WORSHIP
- TO READ QURAAN
- TO OFFER DU'AA
- TO REPENT EVERYDAY
- TO HAVE GOOD CHARACTER

THE MEANING OF LIFE

Sometimes, when you see bad things happening around you, your life isn't going the way you want, or you're feeling a deep sadness that doesn't seem to go away, you start to ask questions.

We often look for the meaning of life and ask big questions about the world around us until we find answers that satisfy our hearts and minds.

Even if you don't consciously do this, you may be able to look back on your life some years later and realize your actions and questions were pointing to your inner desire to find the truth. In Islaam, we understand that this yearning to know why you exist and your inner need to find your purpose comes from the Fitra.

The Fitra is the natural instinct Allaah placed in all of us to worship Him.

Everyone was born as someone who believes in The One God, Allaah, and is in a state of purity with no sin and a yearning for their creator. But it is your parents and/or society that teaches you to become a Muslim, Christian, Jew, other religion, or even someone who is taught not to believe at all.

It is obvious that the Fitra is a real part of the human soul. If it wasn't, how did people of all cultures, countries, regions, and belief systems from the beginning of time to the modern day, some without ever interacting with each other, all come to the conclusion that someone or something must be worshipped? Even those who claim to be atheists or don't follow a religion usually believe in astrology, crystals, or the universe. Because they believe those things will take care of them, effect how their lives turn out, and what will get rid of their trials or attract the things they want towards them; they might not realize it, but this is also a form of religion and worshipping a God.

This shows us that everyone has a natural drive to find out where we fit in the big picture of life and to connect with something greater than ourselves.

Without proper guidance as to which religion or belief is right, many people give up and settle on the conclusion that life is meaningless. They believe we're here simply as the result of evolution and even become angry at who or what they worship. Allaah addresses this way of thinking in the Quraan:

"Did you think that We had created you in play (without any purpose) and that you would not be brought back to Us?" - [Quraan 23:115]

Besides this, some come to the conclusion that since life has no real meaning, and we are born just to die; that we should live life to its fullest based on our own standards and chase our heart's every desire. Allaah also addresses this way of thinking in the Quraan:

"Know that the life of this world is but amusement and diversion and adornment and boasting to one another and competition in increase of wealth and children... And in the Hereafter is severe punishment and forgiveness from Allaah and approval. And what is the worldly life except the enjoyment of delusion." - [Quraan 57:20]

Here, we are reminded that this world is full of entertainment, beauty, amusement, wealth, and enjoyment. But if we live only for pleasure, our lives will feel empty and lonely in the end. We'll wind up chasing unmeaningful fun and even sin, which gets boring after a while, and your heart and soul will still be searching for its true path.

So why are we really here then? What is the true meaning of life, and what is the point of everything happening? Well, Allaah tells us the answer in the Quraan.

> **"I have created the jinn and humankind only for My worship." - [Quraan, 51:56]**

Allaah created us only to worship Him. You may think this answer is simple, but that's the beauty of Islaam, this single action of worshipping Allaah will have a domino effect, and cause your life to become meaningful and purposeful without you even noticing.

To be a Muslim means to submit to Allaah. That means you believe in Him, worship Him, live your life as He commanded, and stay away from what He has forbidden.

If you live your life this way, Allaah will reward you with Jannah. If not, you may have to go to Jahannam or be punished for some time before getting out of it. May Allaah protect us from that, Ameen.

But why follow what Allaah told us to do? Why can't we just live the way we want as long as we don't hurt anyone? Well, You will see in the next part of this chapter how each of the things Allaah commands every Muslim to do helps us live a beautiful life.

Allaah gives us a way of life that causes us to be kind to ourselves and others, and it forces us to think before we act and make decisions that will benefit us in the long run. Islaam is a way of life that keeps you mindful of what's important for your body, your soul, and the people around you. Lastly, it is a way of life that keeps you close to your creator so that when times get tough, you have an explanation, a way to get through it, and Someone to comfort you when no one else can.

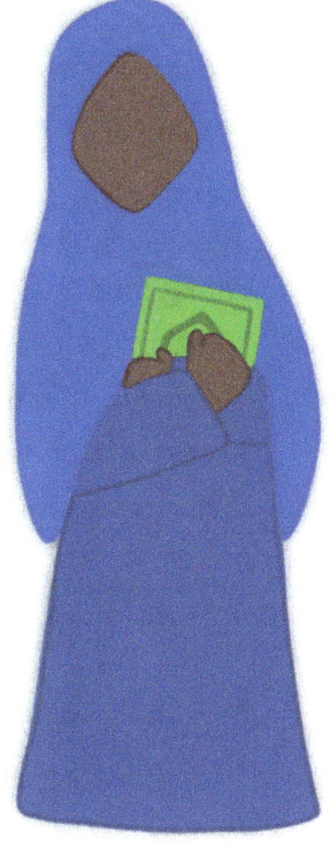

If you simply follow man-made rules or make decisions based on how you feel all the time, you may end up hurting others or yourself, sometimes physically and sometimes mentally.

For example, it is currently a man-made rule in the USA that you can drink alcohol at twenty-one years old. The logic they use is that once you are that age, you can make your own decisions that hopefully won't be irresponsible.

Unfortunately, even adults cannot control themselves when drunk. This leads to bad decision-making, such as saying things they normally wouldn't have and hurting others' feelings, doing risky things like drunk driving, getting into fights, and being especially violent.

In Islaam, no matter the age or occasion, it's Haraam to drink because it takes you out of your stable mind, causes you to act irrationally, and harm yourself and others. Not to mention how unhealthy it is for your body.

This is just one example of how people don't always know what is right or wrong, and making poor decisions can lead to feeling sad, empty, or heartbroken. Life is short, and it's impossible to figure out all the answers on our own before our time ends. That's why we must follow the way Allaah told us to live. He created us, knows everything about us, and understands what's truly best for us.

WHO IS ALLAAH?

Now that you know the meaning of life is to worship Allaah, you need to know Who Allaah is. This is a part of the Fitrah, as mentioned before.

It is a spiritual need to know Allaah because throughout your life, people will come and go, your parents won't be able to take care of you forever, friends come in and out of your life, and sometimes relationships can leave you heartbroken or feeling like nobody's really there for you.

Knowing Allaah will allow your soul to feel like it is always loved, and there is always someone looking out for you. This way, you can feel safe and calm, even when things are not going your way.

To give a brief explanation of Allaah, throughout time, place, and history, there has always been someone or something that people have taken as a God; such as people, idols, animals, objects, and made-up deities to explain the many happenings of life, but there is no God worthy of worship except Allaah.

Allaah is the One true God who created us, all of the universe, and all that exists. He provides for us, cares for us, and has put us on this earth to worship Him. Allaah has been worshipped since the beginning of time and has sent many Prophets and Messengers to teach us how to live and be good people.

Although He has been called different names by different nations, Allaah has always given the same message: to worship Him alone.

Each time a new Prophet was sent, the message was perfected for the new set of people until Allaah sent the final Prophet and Messenger, Muhammad ﷺ.

As Muslims, we follow Islaam, the way of life taught to us through the last Prophet ﷺ, and written for us in the beautiful Quraan, which is the complete, unaltered collection of Allaah's final message to us.

To learn even more about Allaah, let's look at what He says about Himself in the Quraan. We will start with Suratul-Ikhlaas and Ayatul Kursi since these are the most famous descriptions Allaah has given us of Himself.

"Say, He is Allaah, the One. Allaah, the Eternal, Absolute. He does not reproduce, nor was He born. And there is nothing comparable to Him." - [Quraan, 112:1-4]

"Allaah! None has the right to be worshiped but He, the Ever Living, the One Who sustains and protects all that exists. Neither slumber nor sleep overtakes Him. To Him belongs whatever is in the heavens and whatever is on the earth. Who is he that can intercede with Him except with His permission He knows what happens to them (His creatures) in this world, and what will happen to them in the Hereafter. And they will never compass anything of His Knowledge except that which He wills. His throne extends over the heavens and the earth, and He feels no fatigue in guarding and preserving them. And He is the Most High, the Most Great." - [Quraan, 2:255]

In Suratul-Ikhlaas, Allaah gives us an introduction to who He is. Allaah is Al-AHad (The One), meaning there is nothing and no one comparable to Him. He is alone. No one is equal to or like Him in any way. He does not have any children or reproduce. He was also not born or created. He has no beginning and no end. Allaah has and will always exist. Unlike His creation, which, without exception, has an origin and will not last forever, Allaah is without need of anything and is completely independent.

In Ayatul-Kursi, Allaah tells us that He is the only God worthy of worship. He has always existed and will always exist and never die. He takes care of and upholds all that exists. He never gets tired and doesn't need to sleep like we do. Everything on earth, the universe, and beyond into the heavens belongs to Him since He created it. Allaah has complete control over who can hear and speak to Him. He knows what will happen to us in this life and the next, and it is up to Him how much knowledge we will receive. Allaah's throne, meaning His kingdom, which He has full ownership of, extends beyond the heavens and the earth, and He does not get tired of guarding, protecting, and preserving them.

Besides what is said in the Quraan, you can also learn about Allaah by understanding His many names that describe different parts of Who He is. He revealed ninety-nine of them to us throughout the Quraan.

It was narrated by Abu Huraira that our Prophet Muhammad ﷺ said: "There are ninety-nine names of Allaah; he who commits them to memory would get into Paradise." - [Sahih Muslim]

WANT A BEAUTIFUL PDF OF ALLAAH'S 99 NAMES? PULL OUT YOUR CAMERA APP AND SCAN HERE TO GET ONE FOR FREE!

Along with His names and attributes, there are so many stories in the Quraan and Hadeeth that describe things Allaah has done, which allows us to get to know Him even better.

Think of the stories of the Prophets and notable people you learned about growing up. Read their stories again, but this time, look at how Allaah changed their lives, showed them love, care, and mercy, and how He rewarded and took care of them.

Stories like those of Prophet Yusuf, Dawood, and Sulaiman, or those of Uzair, the people of the cave, and the people of the ditch. Read about the stories of those who disbelieved and see how Allaah dealt with them, stories like those of the people of Aad, the people of Prophet Lut, and the uncle Lahab of the Prophet ﷺ. These stories not only give us lessons about how to live our lives but also show us the ways of Allaah.

Another way to learn about Allaah is to think about all He has done for you in your life and the lives of those around you. Think about incidents that have happened where you know it could only have been because of Allaah, or a sign that He was there for you. Ask people around you about their stories and times they realized the things Allaah has done for them or a time when He was especially there for them in times of need.

Never stop thinking about when Allaah has been there for you and others. It is a spiritual need to feel like you will be taken care of, and that there is Someone out there who will always love and be there for you. Always be mindful of Allaah and continue to recognize these moments, Insha Allaah.

Getting to know Allaah is something that will happen throughout your lifetime. It may be easy to learn and memorize the ayaat that describes Him and the ninety-nine names He has revealed to us, but actually understanding them sometimes takes life experiences and trials to fully comprehend. Even then, we will never know everything about Allaah, as there is so much about Him that He has either not revealed to us or that we cannot understand because we have only ever been exposed to worldly things.

OBLIGATORY WORSHIP

As Muslims, we understand that it is not enough to believe in Allaah and keep it in our hearts; instead, we must prove our belief through actions. Believing but not doing anything about it is meaningless since you can fall into a sinful lifestyle where you don't consider how things will affect you or those around you.

Throughout your life, you will have many good days and also many bad, but no matter what, your soul desperately needs to be fed every single day with actions that make it feel good, content, and connected to someone Who cares, that Someone, being Allaah.

This is why Allaah has set obligatory actions for all Muslims who are Mukallaf. These actions are called the Five Pillars of Islaam. They are the five things each Muslim must do no matter what, and they all give your soul a peaceful connection that makes you feel stable and safe. They are:

Shahaadah: - Belief that there is no God worthy of worship except Allaah and that Muhammad ﷺ is His final Messenger. We already went through how belief in Allaah fulfills a spiritual need.

Salaah - As Muslims, we pray five times a day. After belief in Allaah, prayer is the most important thing in a Muslim's life. In fact, if you don't pray at all, most scholars agree that you are no longer a Muslim, and Allaah knows best! What separates a Muslim from a non-Muslim is prayer. Prayer is so serious that even if you don't do any of the other five pillars, wear hijaab, or read Quraan, as long as you still pray and believe in Allaah, you are a Muslim, AlHamdulillaah.

Salaah helps you remember Allaah and feel closer to Him. Throughout the day, it is human nature to constantly make mistakes, and sin. These actions can make you feel heavy, empty, or sad. Every time you pray, Allaah erases your minor sins. When you pray, you focus on the Quraan, praising Allaah and the posture you are in. While praying, you are not allowed to talk, eat, or move around in any way outside of your prayer steps. Because of this, your body is calm as you bow to Allaah while being thoughtful and humble. This constant state of humility and peacefulness keeps your soul feeling fulfilled no matter what else is happening in your life.

Zakaat - In Islaam, it is obligatory for every able Muslim to give a portion of their wealth each year to those who need it. Zakaat is an action that purifies your soul, keeps you mindful of others and the good things in your life, and prevents you from being stingy and selfish. Throughout our lives, we make so many mistakes and sins, and it is a spiritual need to give back and get fulfillment from helping others.

Sawm - Every year, we must fast from food and drink in the month of

Ramadhaan from Fajr to Maghrib prayer. In these Thirty days, we are given a chance to work through and get rid of the spiritual pain, sorrow, and emptiness that might have built up over that year. Fasting in Ramadhaan gives you so many chances to be rid of your sins, build up strong faith, and even change what may have been decreed for you on the night of Qadr. Giving up food, drink, and sins that have become habits gives your mind, body, and soul a much-needed yearly reset.

Hajj - Every year, Muslims from all over the world make the pilgrimage to the Ka'bah in Makkah. If you are able to do so, it is obligatory for every Muslim to make Hajj at least once in their lifetime. Throughout the years, your sins, sorrows, and regrets build up. Your life may not be going the way you hoped, or you may have become disconnected from your religion and need a reset. During Hajj, Allaah completely wipes you of all your sins, and you become as pure as a newborn baby! Free of all previous sins you have committed! Your heart and soul are purified, and with all the sacrifice, hardship, and sincerity Hajj requires, the boost in imaan and blessings you receive will serve you for the rest of your lifetime, Insha Allaah.

> **Abdullah ibn Umar narrated that: "I heard the Messenger of Allaah ﷺ say, 'Islaam has been built on five: testifying that there is no God but Allaah and that Muhammad is the Messenger of Allaah, performing the prayers, paying the Zakaah, making the pilgrimage to the House, and fasting in Ramadan.'" - [al-Bukhaari]**

WEARING HIJAAB

Finally, as a woman, there is an extra obligatory act of worship you must do after becoming mukallaf, and that is wearing hijaab. Allaah tells the believing women to cover themselves in the Quraan, and also specifies who we don't have to cover in front of.

> "And say to the believing women that they should lower their gaze and guard their private parts; that they should not display their beauty and ornaments except what must ordinarily appear thereof; that they should draw their veils over their Juyubihinna (bosoms, bodies) and not display their beauty except to their husbands, their fathers, their husbands' fathers, their sons, their husbands' sons, their brothers, or their brothers' sons or their sisters' sons, or their women or the servants whom their right hands possess, or male servants free of physical needs, or small children who have no sense of the shame of sex, and that they should not strike their feet in order to draw attention to their hidden ornaments. And oh you Believers, turn you all together towards Allaah, that you may attain Bliss." - [Quraan, 24:31]

Here in Suratul-Noor, we get the commandment from Allaah not to display our beauty by covering our entire body and not drawing extra attention through the way we dress and act. We must cover in front of everyone except: Our husbands, fathers, father-in-law, sons, stepsons, brothers, nephews, other women, specific servants, and male children who haven't hit puberty yet. **The reason Muslim women cover is to prevent people who aren't committed to us from seeing or thinking of our bodies in inappropriate ways. If they still do, it's because of their own sick minds, and not based on what they can actually see.**

This ensures that our value comes from our character, and not how we look. For some, it can be hard to dress as Allaah commanded, it's human nature to want to be noticed, complimented, and admired for your beauty. But you should only rely on compliments, admiration, and validation of people who love and care about you, like your friends and family, not strangers. **Pleasing Allaah always comes before pleasing the creation. Even if it's a struggle inside, you will be greatly rewarded, Insha Allaah!**

The human soul aches to be loved and accepted by others. It needs to feel safe and connected to those around it. If people only care about you because you are beautiful, you can start to rely on appearance too much and become insecure about who you are outside of it. You can start to feel like you wouldn't be worth anything if you weren't attractive, and you can even wonder if your friendships or relationships would end if you weren't good-looking.

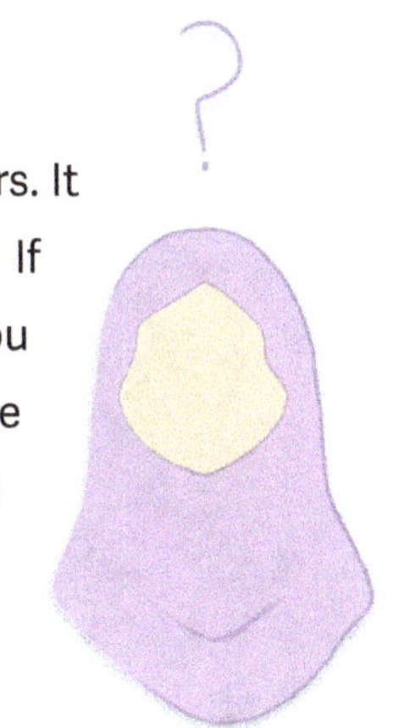

This insecurity can weigh heavy on the soul, and the feeling of not being good enough can make for a sad one. Sometimes, people become obsessed with constantly upping their appearance, even though they were beautiful in the first place. They placed their beauty obsession over their worship, how they treat people, and even learning life skills.

On the other hand, if you feel like you don't look very good or if others treat you badly or in an annoyed fashion just because you aren't the best looking, that can be truly hurtful and impact you for a long time. Especially while going through Puberty, since all emotions are heightened, and this is the time in your life when you will most need to feel connected, accepted, and loved by others. You should never be wrongfully treated or overlooked just because you don't fit the beauty standard. Your worth should never be based on your outward appearance. This can make your insecurities take over your mind, disconnect you from friends, and cause you to feel lonely when there isn't a real reason for it.

As said before, your soul needs to feel secure, connected, and loved by those who matter to stay healthy. This is why it is so important to wear hijaab. Not only does it protect you from strangers thinking of you inappropriately, but it also ensures that your worth comes from your character, not looks.

READING QURAAN

Although listed before are the obligatory acts of worship every Muslim must do, the only ones you have to do on the day to day is prayer, and if you leave the house, covering. Most of the time, our souls need more. We need comforting words, something to soothe us, somewhere to go for answers, and something to feed our souls with extra blessings that connect us closer to Allaah. That is why it is a spiritual need to read the Quraan. The Quraan is Allaah's words, His message to us, and His active miracle.

When you read the Quraan for healing, it will cure your hardened heart with its powerful stories of Allaah's might, compassion, and mercy. It will uplift you when you're feeling low, sad, and depressed by helping you see a path forward and getting words of comfort from your Creator. Even if your problems are not solved after reading, you will feel at ease, calmer, and more peaceful due to the cure Allaah has placed in His Quraan.

It is recommended to have an amount of Quraan you read every single day, no matter what. Depending on how well you can read or how much Quraan you know, start out reading at least three pages a day from the portions you already memorized. This is great for review and will make your past memorization strong so that you don't forget it.

As that becomes easy, build yourself up to five pages, then ten, and then twenty. Although many Muslims still do this, in the West, it has become a nearly abandoned practice. Stay firm in your Imaan and keep peace in your heart by reading a portion of the Quraan every day. You'll be thankful for it on the day of Judgement when the Quraan will be a good proof of you to Allaah so that you can have a better chance at Jannah, insha Allaah!

OFFERING DU'AA

As said before, it is a spiritual need to feel close to Allaah. It gives us such ease to be able to talk to Him, ask for guidance, help, and other needs. Praising Allaah, calling on Him, and knowing He will surely be there for you will ease your mind, give you numerous blessings, and keep you connected to the One who will be there for you when no one else is.

All the Du'aa of the believers are accepted, even if you don't see the result right away. Sometimes we ask for things that Allaah knows is not good for us, so He doesn't let it happen for our protection, but will replace it with something better.

Du'aa is so powerful that Allaah can change what He originally decreed for you because of it.

Always turn to Allaah first; this boosts your imaan, keeps you from being arrogant, and softens your heart. All you have to do is raise your hands and speak with sincerity. If you don't know where to start, there are so many Hadeeth and ayaat in the Quraan that give us Du'aa for our everyday lives and should be memorized and recited when needed.

There is a Du'aa for nearly all everyday actions, from waking up, to eating, leaving the house, using the restroom, getting dressed, traveling, negative feelings, protection, sleep, and much more!

If you would like a collection of authentic Du'aa for everyday use, get the book Husnul-Muslim, (Fortress of the Muslim) or download any free Husnul-Muslim app on your phone.

As for Du'aa where you say whatever you would like to Allaah, even though you can do this at any time and any place (besides the restroom, where you can't say Allaah's name), certain times are special to make it.

+ The last third of the night (Before Fajr)
+ Between the Athaan and Iqaamah
+ When it rains
+ While in Sujood
+ While crying
+ The last hour on Friday (Between Asr and Maghrib)
+ When suffering from oppression

REPENTING EVERYDAY

Allaah created us to be flawed individuals. The test for us lies in overcoming our flaws and being righteous believers despite them so that we can get to Jannah, Insha Allaah. It is human nature to sin and make many mistakes every day, but the only way we will be punished for those actions is if we don't repent.

Repentance is turning to Allaah sincerely, asking His forgiveness, and intending not to do it again. Allaah is Al-Ghafoor (The most forgiving) and will always forgive us, no matter what.

Even if you commit a sin over and over and feel hopeless that you will never be able to stop, always continue asking Allaah's forgiveness. Never assume that Allaah is not accepting your repentance, even if you have an addiction to something Haraam, and do it every single day.

That way of thinking is the trick of Shaytaan, who wants you to become disconnected from Allaah. If you still believe that Allaah is not accepting your repentance, remember that He is Al-Ghafoor, and to assume He cannot forgive you is a major insult to Him, since Allaah is capable of all things.

> **"Say: Oh my servants! Who have acted extravagantly against their own souls, do not despair of the mercy of Allaah; surely Allaah forgives the faults altogether; surely He is the Forgiving the Merciful." - [Quraan 39:53]**

Remember that when you sin, you are bringing down your own soul and diminishing your chances of making it to Jannah. Our bad deeds can make us depressed, sad, angry, regretful, and hurt. They can weigh on us like bricks and keep us from being our best selves. This is why repentance is a spiritual need; you must free yourself from bad deeds that weigh you down and hinder your life.

> **"And whoever does evil or acts unjustly to his soul, then asks forgiveness of Allaah, he shall find Allaah Forgiving, Merciful" - [Quraan 4:110]**

The best way to make things right after committing a sin is to do a good deed after repenting. If you do this, Allaah will change your bad deed into a good one.

> **"Except him who repents and believes and does a good deed; so these are they of whom Allaah changes the evil deeds to good ones; and Allaah is Forgiving, Merciful." - [Quraan 25:70]**

It is crucial to repent as soon as you make a mistake. Always ask for forgiveness right away after a bad deed, since you may forget later or never end up repenting. You can only repent for your sins until you die, and since we never know when that will happen, we must repent every day without haste.

> **"And return to your Lord time after time and submit to Him before there comes to you the punishment, then you shall not be helped." - [Quraan, 39:54]**

Even though our Prophet Muhammad ﷺ was the best person to walk this earth, he still repented one hundred times every day. Take his example and always ask for forgiveness; never assume you are above that; and do it with sincerity. Allaah will always accept it, and continue to be there and take care of you.

HAVING GOOD CHARACTER

Last on the list, but definitely not least important, is having good character. Good character is often overlooked in our society, where being righteous, moral, kind, and humble isn't valued as much. Instead, people often value wealth, beauty, and the ability to entertain others, even if it means acting in ways that humiliate themselves.

However, dear reader, you must always keep in mind the reason you are on this earth, and that is to worship Allaah so you can get to Jannah, Insha Allaah.

This Hadeeth teaches us that having good character is an absolute must if you want to make it to Jannah. It is a spiritual need to be a good charactered person because the opposite of that is being immoral, treating people unjustly, and being selfish. All those things weigh down on our souls, disconnect us from Allaah, and cause harm to others.

For example, a person can pray their five prayers, recite Quraan every day, wear hijaab, and even fast for extra days, but still go to the Hellfire! How? By committing major sins that come from bad character, such as gossiping, slandering, showing off, oppressing others, and making money off of Haraam such as Zinaa or alcohol.

Having good character will prevent you from committing major sins like these and keep you closely connected with Allaah as well as your family and friends. Keep in mind that you will be questioned on the Day of Judgement for every single moment of your life, not just the worship you did, so it is important to have good character at all times, even when alone.

> "On the Day when every soul will come disputing for itself, and every soul will be fully compensated for what it did, and they will not be wronged." - [Quraan 16:111]

Although perfecting your character is something you will be doing for the rest of your life, understanding what good character is can help you progress more quickly; especially if you approach it as an act of worship to get into Jannah.

So what is good character in Islaam? To answer this, you must look to our Prophet Muhammad ﷺ as he is the best of examples.

> "Verily, you (Oh Muhammad) are upon great moral character." - [Quraan, 68:4]

Even before becoming Allaah's Messenger, Muhammad ﷺ was an honest man who had earned the name al-Amin (the trustworthy) from those who knew him. Our Prophet Muhammad ﷺ was kind to everyone, no matter who they were or where they came from. He was humble in speech and in the way he lived despite having the status of king before his death. He was generous with whatever Allaah blessed him with. Muhammad ﷺ was always concerned for others above himself; he would pray for his nation every day, and practiced what he preached more diligently than anyone else.

Qataadah narrated that: I said to Aisha, "Oh mother of the believers, tell me about the character of the Messenger of Allaah, ﷺ." Aisha said, "Have you not read the Quraan?" I said, "Of course." Aisha said, "Verily, the character of the Prophet of Allaah was the Quraan." - [Sahih Muslim]

But don't just take my word for it. Learn about the Prophet ﷺ for yourself. Read his biography and learn the Hadeeths of his kindness towards others, animals, slaves, and even prisoners of war. Learn about how he would do chores at home and distribute his last to those in need, how he never spoke harshly or with foul language, did not like being praised, and put Allaah first no matter what. Learn about his mercy even towards the disbelievers, like the people of Taif, who, despite stoning him out of their village, the Prophet ﷺ asked for them not to be punished. Read about our Messenger ﷺ and apply his good qualities to your own personality and actions.

"For you in the Messenger of Allaah is the finest example to follow..." - [Quraan, 33:21]

DEALING WITH FEELINGS

Now that you're in a tricky spot between being a kid and becoming an adult, you'll start to dream about what you want your life to look like, even if you can't make it all happen just yet. Everything around you, from what happens day to day to the people you meet, and the things they say, begins to take on new meaning. You'll find new things that interest you and become deeply attached to them. You'll make new friends and connect with them on a closer level than you would before. Suddenly, when you feel emotions like anger, sadness, worry, hope, or happiness, the feeling is overwhelming.

Along with complicated family matters, school pressures, and the need to find your place with those around you, going through Puberty can be pretty tough.

Although you might feel all over the place right now, it will get better, Insha Allaah. Your mind is changing to prepare you for adult life, and although the process may be rocky, there's a lot of good waiting for you on this journey, Insha Allaah.

WHY DO I GET MOOD SWINGS?

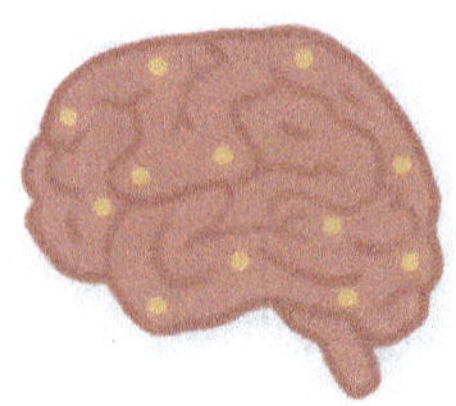

When your body starts producing the hormones that trigger Puberty, not only do physical symptoms happen, but emotional ones too—estrogen, testosterone, and progesterone cause you to crave emotional experiences and intensify your feelings towards them.

At the same time, you also might start to look for approval from people your age outside of your family, wanting to spend more time with friends and peers. This is a natural part of growing up, helping you prepare for starting your own family one day and finding a community that will welcome and support you as an adult.

Your prefrontal cortex—the part of the brain responsible for making decisions and controlling emotions—doesn't fully develop until you're twenty-five years old; so during Puberty, your emotions might become overwhelming all while your brain is still learning how to handle them.

This can lead to taking risks, becoming more assertive, and forming strong opinions you didn't have before. It might also make you more passionate, excited, and loving. With all of this happening in your brain at once, it's no wonder your mood may be all over the place.

HAVING A CRUSH

As you get older, you observe the world and meet more people. You get swept up in the world of your peers and crave more connection from those around you. It's almost unavoidable that you'll come to have romantic feelings for that special someone at least once in your life.

Having a crush is a natural part of life. It's human nature to crave romantic relationships, but there is a proper way of going about them.

If you're too young to get married, there is absolutely nothing you can do about having a crush except dreaming and praying about it. As Muslims, men and women can't touch, hug, kiss, or intimately talk to the opposite gender unless they're related, or married to each other. When a girl has a crush, there are certain things she might want to do to impress the guy she likes, some are alright under the right conditions, but others are not; let's examine the main five.

ONE - CHANGING UP YOUR LOOK

This includes choices like wearing makeup, perfume, and dressing in ways you feel are more attractive. It's important for Muslim girls to know that wearing makeup outside the home or in front of men who are non-Mahram is not permitted. This is because hijaab isn't just about covering, but also making sure not to beautify yourself for people who are not committed to you.

You can always dress better and change your style if you want of course, but you have to meet all the conditions of hijaab and keep your outfits Halaal. Although we will learn about them in detail in a later chapter, here is a quick list of the conditions of hijaab:

- ✦ The hijaab must cover the entire body
- ✦ It should conceal everything underneath it
- ✦ It must be loose-fitting
- ✦ It must not be perfumed
- ✦ It should not be overly adorned
- ✦ It should not be extravagant and vain
- ✦ It should not resemble mens clothing
- ✦ It should not resemble non-Muslim clothing

Remember that a Muslim should never walk around looking unkempt, dirty, or mismatched, and your clothes should always be clean, matching, and presentable, no matter what. Looking your best shouldn't depend on impressing a guy, it's already a part of being a well kept Muslim who takes good care of themselves.

TWO - CONVERSATION

As Muslim women, we can't intimately talk to men we aren't related or married to without a Mahram (your male guardian) around. This is because people easily connect through conversation and may end up talking romantically in ways that aren't appropriate if left alone.

When you're old enough to think about marriage, and your Mahram says it's okay, you can talk normally and have friendly chats with the intention of getting to know someone for marriage. Until then, it's important to steer clear of private talks, including messaging or commenting on social media posts. Just like in real life, replying to stories and chatting online is a way of connecting through conversation, so the rule applies there, too.

Ibn Abbaas narrated that: "I heard Allaahs Messenger ﷺ delivering a sermon and making this observation: 'No person should be alone with a woman except when there is a Mahram with her, and the woman should not undertake journey except with a Mahram...' - [Sahih Muslim]

THREE - ACTING OUT

Sometimes while having a crush, we might do things to get their attention that we wouldn't normally do. Like laughing louder at a joke when they're nearby, doing something silly when a lot of people are watching, joining groups we're not really interested in just because they're there, or jumping into conversations just so they can hear us talk.

These things aren't Haraam of course, but acting differently to gain someone's attention may lead to many embarrassing, awkward, and cringey moments. We might end up saying things we wish we could take back, and often, these efforts don't make the person like us more.

Having Hayaa (shyness/modesty) is an important part of being a Muslim for both men and women, as said in these ayaat:

> **"Say to the believing men that they should lower their gaze and guard their modesty: that will make for greater purity for them: And Allaah is All-Aware of what they do. And say to the believing women that they should lower their gaze and guard their modesty..."** - [Quraan, 24:30-31]

A part of having Hayaa is avoiding acting out for attention, as mentioned later in the same ayah:

> **"...and that they should not strike their feet in order to draw attention to their hidden ornaments..."** [Quraan, 24:31]

So instead, be your true, interesting, and wonderful self. Don't go out of your way to impress others, especially if it brings you out of your real personality. Have Hayaa, and build friendships with people who cherish you for you! When the time comes, Allaah will give you the right partner who will love you best when you're being yourself, Insha Allaah.

FOUR - DAYDREAMING

Daydreaming is completely normal and Halaal, even in Islaam, Allaah does not judge us by our thoughts, but by our actions instead. However, it's important to keep our daydreams in check so they don't lead to unhappiness, bad decision making, or Haraam actions. In fact, if your imagination is leading you to these things, it was recommended by our Prophet ﷺ to fast.

> **Abu Huraira narrated that the Messenger of Allaah ﷺ said: "… Fasting is a shield from the fire and from committing sins…" - [al-Bukhaari]**

As long as it isn't causing you any harm as stated before, you can dream to your hearts content. Just remember that imagining someone as perfect in your head might make you overlook that they're actually quite different in real life, and may not be the person you built them up to be in your imagination.

FIVE - SEEKING ONLINE ADVICE

The first thing most of us do when we have questions is look online for answers. For day to day things that's okay, but your views on religion, relationships, and mental health should never be taken from Google, YouTube Videos, or short form content (like Tik Tok, YouTube Shorts, or Reels). They are good aids with little reminders and tips that may help here and there but should never be taken at face value. Usually, the advice and information needs to be investigated before you can accept it as true.

When looking for advice about relationships, it's important to remember that non-Muslims giving it have a completely different way of going about them than us. Most of their tactics are Haraam, and lead to heartbreak and bad decision making in the end.

Always choose Allaah's way over the people's, even if you're really tempted to do it. By putting Allaah first, you're not only earning blessings but are also promised something much better in return. Remember, dear reader, that the person you like in middle and high school is most likely not the person you will end up with. People change, move, and are taken in different directions by life. For this reason, it is even more important that you don't do Haraam to impress or be with someone; on top of earning bad deeds, it's giving too much of yourself for someone who won't be in your life to stay.

Always ask Allaah to make things easy for you when the right person comes along. When you grow to a marriageable age, your parents and peers will guide you through what you need to have a good relationship, and you can read books, ask married people, and see what Islaam has to say about it. If you ask Allaah for help in the romance department, He will surely guide you, so don't stress, and seek advice from people who put Allaah first.

DEALING WITH ANGER

Growing up is hard. You're coming into a whole new version of yourself while having to keep up with expectations, responsibilities, new friendships, and sometimes family issues. During Puberty, you may be overwhelmed and frustrated by things more easily, and anger can be a lot more intense. Sometimes it's warranted, other times, not so much. Anger is a normal and needed emotion; but there is a proper way to express it.

One of the biggest reasons for anger during Puberty is when things aren't going your way. We're often told that our teenage years should be full of fun, but sometimes, it doesn't work out that way. Maybe your parents don't let you hang out as much as you'd like, they seem more critical, friendships are harder to maintain, family issues might be weighing you down, and school is becoming more stressful. You start to think no one understands you, and it becomes harder to express how you feel.

It's okay to be upset about those things. However, if you let anger build up without properly dealing with it, you'll end up expressing it in ways that hurt others and weigh down on your heart and mind. So, how should Muslims deal with anger?

KEEP SILENT

During arguments, parents scolding you, friends being hurtful, or siblings disrespecting your boundaries, its easy to lose self control and say things you'll regret later.

Whether it be talking back or disrespecting a parent, cursing at your siblings, or telling your friends off, you'll find in the end it wasn't worth it, didn't solve anything, made you look like the bad guy, and now you've said something you can't take back. **Remember, you'll never regret choosing to stay quiet.** It's not easy, but keeping your angry thoughts to yourself is often the wisest choice.

Keep in mind that by staying quiet, you'll also be able to listen better. This will allow you to see the other person's side and sometimes discover that you may have been wrong.

Ibn Abbaas narrated that the Messenger of Allaah ﷺ said: "If any of you becomes angry, let him keep silent." - [Sahih Albaani]

Whenever you're angry, you become vulnerable to Shaytaan, who wants to use your negative feelings against you. Say the isti'aathah (A'oothu-billaahi min-ashaytaan-irrajeem) over and over, even if it has to be under your breath. Breathe and ask Allaah to give you patience and guide you to do the right thing for that situation.

> **Sulayman ibn Sard narrated that: "I was sitting with the Prophet ﷺ, and two men were slandering one another. One of them was red in the face, and the veins on his neck were standing out. The Prophet ﷺ said, 'I know a word which, if he were to say it, what he feels would go away. If he said "I seek refuge with Allaah from the Shaytaan," what he feels (his anger) would go away.'" - [al-Bukhaari]**

THINK AHEAD

If you disrespect your family or hurt your friends, think about what will come of it. How did they react the last time there was a heated situation or when you spoke out the wrong way? If what you do will have more bad results than good, it's not worth it. Remember also that Allaah rewards us for refraining from acting out of frustration. But if you disrespect your parents or wrong someone out of anger, you will get bad deeds and may have to pay on the day of judgment. May Allaah protect us from that, Ameen.

LEAVE RESPECTFULLY

Depending on the situation, it can be disrespectful to walk away. If a parent, teacher, or elder is scolding you, this would not be the correct thing to do.

Instead, wait until they are finished speaking and respectfully walk away afterward. If it is a friend or sibling you are arguing with, tell them you need a moment, and then take your leave. Never walk away while yelling, stomping, being aggressive, or slamming things, since that just means you're throwing a tantrum and ruining your chances of anyone taking you seriously.

SWITCH YOUR POSITION

Ever hear someone need to give bad news and say "Are you sitting down?" or "You'll want to sit down for this." Well, in Islaam, if you find yourself feeling angry while standing up, you should sit or lay down if sitting to calm yourself, as said in this Hadeeth:

> **The Messenger of Allaah ﷺ said: "If any of you becomes angry and he is standing, let him sit down, so his anger will go away; if it does not go away, let him lie down." - [Abu Dawood]**

OFFER WUDHOO

Wudhoo is not only a physical cleaning but a spiritual one too. Offering wudhoo will keep Shaytaan away and allow you a chance to calm down in a spiritual state.

REFLECT

When you are so angry about a situation that it stays on your mind all day, or in cases where you may have been wrong, it's time to reflect. **To reflect is to ask Allaah for guidance, think, and look at the facts as evidence of what really happened.** Doing this will allow you to see things from a broader perspective and with a deeper level of understanding than you had before.

JOURNAL

Write down why you're angry, make a video diary (even if you delete it later), or a voice recording to vent. This will help get things off your chest and give you a chance to find some relief. If you don't find a way to let out and express your feelings, the anger will go away for a little while but stay building up in your chest until after many days, weeks, months, or even years, you explode.

TALK IT OUT

As said before, if you let your anger build up, it will only lead to an explosion later on, so venting to someone can be very helpful. **However, keep in mind that we are Muslims, and backbiting is Haraam.** If you wish to tell someone about a situation you're angry about, do not make what happened seem worse than it was; don't talk badly about others who were involved and only mention what they did without adding insults or negative talk about them. Do not vent to too many people. Only one or two people who don't gossip and will give you good advice, help, or relief from the situation.

Never take anger out physically by hitting, pushing, slapping, or punching, including on yourself. Remember, dear reader, your body is a gift from Allaah, and it's your duty to care for it. If you allow yourself to take out your anger with violence as a teen, you may become a violent adult, which is immature and dangerous for both yourself and others. Remember, healthily managing your anger is a sign of maturity and respect for yourself and others.

SADNESS AND DEPRESSION

During Puberty, girls experience a heightened sense of negative emotion. It's not known exactly why. You might feel sad because of things happening in your life, experiences you've had, or because of words others have said to or about you. Maybe you feel sad because things are tough, or you don't have any control over what's happening, which makes you feel helpless. Perhaps you just aren't happy with yourself, or how your life is turning out. These are all reasons a person can be sad, but sometimes, this sadness can turn into something deeper: depression.

Depression is a mental illness that many people have. It is when your mind is stuck in a constant cycle of deep sadness to the point where you are always either crying or completely numb about what's hurting you. It can last for months or even years, and finding a way out of it can be hard. Depression is not easy to escape, and the way to heal it is different for everyone. But here are some things you can do to make things much easier for yourself if you struggle with it. If you don't have depression but get deeply sad, these tips will help you too, Insha Allaah.

TURN TO ALLAAH

No matter what, always turn to Allaah first. Ask Him to ease you of your pain or suffering, to take away what is causing you sadness, and to help you through whatever hardship you're going through. Pray to Him, cry to Him, and always remember Him. Even if you've been asking for help for years and feel like your prayers aren't being accepted, remember that is the trick of the Shaytaan, and your prayers are always working, just on Allaah's time, not yours. Sometimes, Allaah will solve your problem quickly, and sometimes it will take a long time.

Human beings learn and grow through experience, and sometimes the experiences are painful. This life is a test, and if you pass (despite the hardships) you will be accepted into Jannah, Insha Allaah. Sometimes, you must go through hard times to become a better person or turn back to Allaah. Hard times are unavoidable, so make it easier on yourself, and never stop turning to Him! Here are some Du'aas to protect you from, and pull you out of a depressive slump. When sad, say them over and over until you feel better.

اللّهُـمَّ إِنِّي أَعُوذُ بِكَ مِنَ الهَـمِّ وَ الْحُـزْنِ، والعَجـزِ والكَسَلِ والبُخْـلِ والجُـبْنِ، وضَلـعِ الـدَّيْنِ وغَلَبَـةِ الرِّجال

"Oh Allaah, I seek refuge in you from grief and sadness, from weakness and from laziness, from miserliness and from cowardice, from being overcome by debt and overpowered by men." - [Al-Bukhaari]

اللّهُمَّ إِنِّي عَبْدُكَ، ابْنُ عَبْدِكَ، ابْنُ أَمَتِكَ، نَاصِيَتِي بِيَدِكَ، مَاضٍ فِيَّ حُكْمُكَ، عَدْلٌ فِيَّ قَضَاؤُكَ، أَسْأَلُكَ بِكُلِّ اسْمٍ هُوَ لَكَ سَمَّيْتَ بِهِ نَفْسَكَ، أَوْ أَنْزَلْتَهُ فِي كِتَابِكَ، أَوْ عَلَّمْتَهُ أَحَدًا مِنْ خَلْقِكَ، أَوِ اسْتَأْثَرْتَ بِهِ فِي عِلْمِ الْغَيْبِ عِنْدَكَ، أَنْ تَجْعَلَ الْقُرْآنَ رَبِيعَ قَلْبِي، وَنُورَ صَدْرِي، وَجَلَاءَ حُزْنِي، وَذَهَابَ هَمِّي

"Oh Allaah! Indeed I am Your servant Son of Your male servant and female servant, My forelock is in Your Hand, And Your Judgment upon me is assured, and Your Decree upon me is just, I ask you with every name that You have named Yourself with, or revealed in Your Book (Quraan), or taught to any of Your creation, or kept with Yourself in the knowledge of the unseen that is with You, that you make the Quraan the life of my heart, and the light of my chest and the banisher of my sadness and the reliever of my distress." - [Ahmed]

اللَّهُمَّ رَحْمَتَكَ أَرْجُو فَلاَ تَكِلْنِي إِلَى نَفْسِي طَرْفَةَ عَيْنٍ وَأَصْلِحْ لِي شَأْنِي كُلَّهُ لاَ إِلَهَ إِلاَّ أَنْتَ

"Oh Allaah! I hope for your mercy. Do not abandon me to myself even for the blink of an eye, correct for me all my affairs. There is none worthy of worship except you." - [Abu Dawood]

حَسْبِيَ ٱللَّهُ لَا إِلَهَ إِلَّا هُوَ ۖ عَلَيْهِ تَوَكَّلْتُ ۖ وَهُوَ رَبُّ ٱلْعَرْشِ ٱلْعَظِيمِ

"Sufficient for me is Allaah; there is no deity worthy of worship except Him. On Him I have relied, and He is the Lord of the Mighty Throne." - [Quraan, 9:129]

REFLECT

Reflect to find out why you are sad or depressed and where to go from there. Sometimes, your sadness and depression come from things you don't have control over, but if you just sit in sadness without trying to get out of it, you might find yourself stuck in it until you decide to do something.

To reflect is to ask Allaah for guidance, think, look at the facts as evidence of what really happened, and write down your thoughts. Doing this will allow you to see things from a broader perspective and give you a deeper level of understanding you hadn't had before.

SAY THE MORNING AND EVENING ATHKAAR

The morning and evening Athkaar are a collection of Du'aas for protection from yourself, others, disbelief, Shaytaan, and calamity, rectifying your affairs, asking forgiveness, thanking Allaah, protection on the day of judgment, and much more! Believe in the help Allaah has given you, dear reader, and keep it in your life. You will find much relief from it, Insha Allaah.

TALK TO SOMEONE YOU TRUST

Talk to a friend or family member who has shown they care for you. If you keep everything inside, you could overthink, and the problem might hurt much deeper than needed. You may see things differently after voicing your sadness out loud and find some relief from the heaviness that has built up inside you.

This may be hard for some people because they might be embarrassed or feel like it's not worth it. You're only human, and as a social creature, a part of healing is connecting with others. People are a lot more similar to each other than you might think. If you have struggled with something, chances are someone you know has, too. They might be able to use their experience to help or simply to be a comforting shoulder to cry on.

No matter what you're going through, dear reader, you are not alone. Take a chance and talk to someone who loves you, Insha Allaah.

If you have too many thoughts and don't know who to turn to after Allaah, write them down in a private book or on a diary app that locks. Putting your thoughts on paper or typing them out can provide a sense of relief, especially on days when you're overwhelmed with sadness. Think of your journal as a safe and private space where you can let your honest thoughts and emotions flow.

NEVER TALK BADLY ABOUT YOURSELF!

Some people are depressed because they have a low self-image of themselves. Instead of seeing all their wonderful qualities, they focus on their flaws and believe that is all they really are. Instead of believing they can change and become better or that they have more good qualities than bad, they are stuck in a cycle of sadness and hopelessness, thinking they are not worth anything, and don't deserve good for themselves.

As a result, they talk badly about themselves to others, saying things like, "I'm so dumb." "Ew, I'm so ugly." or "It doesn't matter because I deserve this bad thing anyway."

This is negative self-talk and a very dangerous habit for your mind. Sure, you shouldn't think you're too good to fail or be too blind to see when you aren't at your best, but it is damaging to label yourself as negative things in your brain.

Nothing lasts forever, no one is ever at their best or their worst or even normal forever. The difference between humans and animals, and why Allaah raised us above the rest of creation, is because of our intellect. The human mind is capable of much more than we give it credit for. If you tell yourself you are ugly, annoying, worthless, a failure, stupid, etc, you are limiting your mind to thinking that is who you truly are and that it can't escape. You're not giving your mind a chance to see beyond those labels.

Even if you believe these negative things about yourself, never negatively self talk, whether it be to others, or even yourself. Your body does what your mind says, and if you stop thinking and saying negativity about yourself, your mind will be free to change and accomplish so much more.

> **"Don't speak negatively about yourself, even as a joke. Your body doesn't know the difference... Change the way you speak about yourself and you can change your life. What you're not changing you're also choosing." - Bruce Lee**

Don't stop caring just because it's about you. **You are worthy of love, kindness, and respect. If Allaah loves you, who are you not to do the same?** Choose to see the good in you over your flaws, and see how your mind changes for the better, Insha Allaah!

THERAPY

Although it's the first thing you should do after turning to Allaah, this is later on the list because if you're young, your parents are in charge of getting you into it. Sometimes therapy is not accessible for families to get, as it can be expensive, or some people may not believe it will really work.

Always ask Allaah to make it easy for you to get the help you need. If you are sad all the time, numb to your life, don't care about yourself, or are always going through hard things, you should definitely get therapy. Whether it be online or in person, therapists are trained to listen, care for, and give solutions to problems we can't see our way out of.

BE GRATEFUL

Life is tough. Sometimes things get overwhelming, and bad stuff happens. But in the end, there is always something to be grateful for. In situations where your depression isn't caused by something jeopardizing your life and safety, choose to be grateful over sad.

Focusing too much on the negatives, like things not going as planned or feeling burdened by too many thoughts, is easy. But it's important to do the hard thing and consciously choose to think of what you're thankful for instead.

Every day write down at least one thing you are grateful for in your life, such as Allaah, health, someone you love, not being hungry, being in a safe country, a safe home, your family, friends, etc. Then reflect on those things and thank Allaah for them. You will find this settles your heart a little each day.

Remember, dear reader, that things could always be worse and nothing lasts forever; this time of hardship and sadness will pass, Insha Allaah. Show Allaah you are grateful and He will give you so much more.

ANXIETY AND OVERWHELMING THOUGHTS

Getting nervous, overthinking, and feeling worried are all normal emotions that you'll get from time to time. But when your thoughts are so overwhelming that you are always worried, in fear, paranoid, and having physical reactions, this is anxiety. You breathe too fast, your heart is racing, your stomach is queasy, you may become dizzy, have pounding headaches, and not be able to sleep at night, all because your negative thoughts have taken over your body and put you in an overwhelming state of worry and fear. Anxiety is when your mind's worries are taking a physical toll on your body.

During Puberty, you may become more anxious than ever before. Sometimes life is stressful and can lead to higher anxiousness, however, a lot of the reason for your spike in anxiety is likely because of your hormones.

Allopregnanolone is a steroid your body releases in stressful situations to calm you down, but during Puberty, it has the opposite effect, making you more anxious.

Because anxiety comes from a negative state of mind, the way to heal from it is similar to the way you heal from depression. However, some steps are specifically meant for treating anxiety.

TURN TO ALLAAH

Anxiety comes from fear and overthinking. When you train your mind to remember that Allaah is in control and He will protect you from the bad outcomes you are afraid of, your body will feel more at ease and place less pressure on yourself for things that are out of your control.

Turning to Allaah means to submit to Him and understand that He will take care of you no matter what. Here are three Du'aas that should be said over and over when anxious, until you feel better.

اللَّهُمَّ رَحْمَتَكَ أَرْجُو فَلاَ تَكِلْنِي إِلَى نَفْسِي طَرْفَةَ عَيْنٍ وَأَصْلِحْ لِي شَأْنِي كُلَّهُ لاَ إِلَهَ إِلاَّ أَنْتَ

"Oh Allaah! I hope for your mercy. Do not abandon me to myself even for the blink of an eye, correct for me all my affairs. There is none worthy of worship except you." - [Abu Dawood]

اللَّهُمَّ إِنِّي عَبْدُكَ، ابْنُ عَبْدِكَ، ابْنُ أَمَتِكَ، نَاصِيَتِي بِيَدِكَ، مَاضٍ فِيَّ حُكْمُكَ، عَدْلٌ فِيَّ قَضَاؤُكَ، أَسْأَلُكَ بِكُلِّ اسْمٍ هُوَ لَكَ سَمَّيْتَ بِهِ نَفْسَكَ، أَوْ أَنْزَلْتَهُ فِي كِتَابِكَ، أَوْ عَلَّمْتَهُ أَحَدًا مِنْ خَلْقِكَ، أَوِ اسْتَأْثَرْتَ بِهِ فِي عِلْمِ الْغَيْبِ عِنْدَكَ، أَنْ تَجْعَلَ الْقُرْآنَ رَبِيعَ قَلْبِي، وَنُورَ صَدْرِي، وَجَلَاءَ حُزْنِي، وَذَهَابَ هَمِّي

"Oh Allaah! Indeed I am Your servant Son of Your male servant and female servant, My forelock is in Your Hand, And Your Judgment upon me is assured, and Your Decree upon me is just, I ask you with every name that You have named Yourself with, or revealed in Your Book (Quraan), or taught to any of Your creation, or kept with Yourself in the knowledge of the unseen that is with You, that you make the Quraan the life of my heart, and the light of my chest and the banisher of my sadness and the reliever of my distress." - [Ahmed]

حَسْبِيَ ٱللَّهُ لَا إِلَٰهَ إِلَّا هُوَ ۖ عَلَيْهِ تَوَكَّلْتُ ۖ وَهُوَ رَبُّ ٱلْعَرْشِ ٱلْعَظِيمِ

"Sufficient for me is Allaah; there is no deity worthy of worship except Him. On Him I have relied, and He is the Lord of the Mighty Throne." - [Quraan, 9:129]

SAY THE MORNING AND EVENING ATHKAAR

Again, the morning and evening Athkaar really help. This is because the Du'aa's include asking for protection against things you may be anxious over, as well as protection from yourself, others, disbelief, Shaytaan, and calamity, rectifying your affairs, asking forgiveness, thanking Allaah, protection on the day of judgment, and much more. You can find them in the book or free app, Husnul Muslim, as well as by scanning the barcode on the next page!

TAKE CONTROL AND CHANGE YOUR THOUGHTS

If you allow your thoughts to take over your life, you will be stuck in a constant state of anxiety without hope of getting out. You have to choose not to let your mind race and take control of it before it gets out of hand.

What separates humans from animals and the rest of creation is our intellect and the power Allaah gave us to choose how we will live our lives. Never allow negative thinking and the whispers of the Shaytaan to make you think you can't take control of your mind. Allaah gave you this special gift, you just have to believe, to use it.

Before the negative thoughts overwhelm you, catch yourself and say out loud, "NO!" Then, purposely change what you are thinking to something more logical or positive.

For example, if you're in fear of messing up a presentation for school, instead of allowing your mind to say, "They're gonna laugh." "You're about to get roasted." "You probably look so dumb right now." "You're gonna mess up and look stupid."

Say out loud, "NO!" Then, force yourself to remember how hard you worked on the presentation. You know what it's about. You know what to say. Remember what happened when your classmate gave their presentation and stuttered? No one laughed. They barely noticed. You look just fine, and no one is putting pressure on you. In their heads, they're just watching, as you did for them. Everything is going to be okay.

Ask Allaah to make the task easy and successful for you. Even if you have an embarrassing moment, other people will likely forget about it in a couple of days or weeks and let it go. Do not put so much pressure on yourself, and remember that others are not out to get you.

When it comes to anxiety, if you change your thoughts, you change your life.

BREATHE AND SAY THE ISTI'AATHAH

Yes, anxiety is a mental illness, but Shaytaan certainly makes it worse. He sniffs out our weakest spots and plays on our thoughts and emotions to make things seem worse than they truly are. When you are feeling anxious, say the isti'aathah (A'oothu Billaahi minashaytaan irajeem), and breathe slowly in through your nose and out through your mouth.

PRAY

Salaah is a calming way to worship. With the repetitive motions, Quraan, Athkaar, and having to keep your mind on Allaah instead of your fears, it will certainly calm an anxious mind. If you skip your five prayers or don't pray them on time, you will find your heart heavy and develop a void only Allaah can fill. This heaviness contributes to a mind in turmoil and makes anxiety worse.

READ QURAAN

The Quraan is medicine for the soul. It feeds your heart peace and ease, which in turn calms your mind. While reading Quraan, your mind is on the words and off of your worries and fears. Read it in Arabic to gain blessings, and read the Tafseer and explanation for understanding.

The more you know about it, the more you will find a true companion in it.

STAY BUSY

A mind with nothing to do is a mind easily overwhelmed by thoughts. If there is nothing to keep it busy, your thoughts have more time to build and take over. This is why staying busy is so important.

Scrolling on social media and watching your favorite entertainment is not a way to keep your mind busy. It is an empty distraction that only keeps you invested for as long as the screen is on.

Healthier ways of distracting yourself can be:

+ Having a hobby like writing stories and poetry, drawing, making jewelry, sewing, clay sculpting, knitting, crocheting, trying new recipes, etc.
+ Helping your family around the house.
+ Connecting with friends by calling or hanging out with them.
+ Reading Quraan.
+ Joining a class after school for something you like.
+ Spending time with animals
+ Volunteering for things that will help your community.

AVOID CAFFEINE

Food or drinks with caffeine in them increase feelings of anxiety. This is because caffeine indirectly triggers neurotransmitters like norepinephrine, dopamine, and serotonin. All are chemicals that affect the body and mind and can cause your heart to race. When an anxious person's heart races, it can trigger fear and overwhelming thoughts since that is what usually causes it. Stay away from coffee and energy drinks, and check the labels on certain teas, other drinks, and sweets for caffeine.

THE 333 METHOD

Sometimes anxiety can become so overwhelming that your mind drifts out of reality and fear takes over in a physical way; causing your heart to race, body to tremble, and tears to become uncontrollable. In times like these, it helps to ground yourself in reality and get out of your head. The 3 3 3 method can be used to calm you down; here is how you do it:

✦ Name 3 things you see
✦ Point out 3 sounds you hear
✦ Name 3 parts of your body or 3 moving things in your environment

After this, you must continuously recite your anxiety Du'aas, breathe, and talk things out with someone you trust.

TAKE A GHUSL

A ghusl is like a spiritual bath. It is a full version of wudhoo that calms the soul and washes away the weight of the day. If your mind and heart are racing, taking a ghusl will help calm you down.

SLEEP WELL

If you don't get enough sleep, your anxiety can get much worse because your mind hasn't had enough rest. This can be hard for some because anxious thoughts often keep you awake. Say your Du'aas, take a ghusl, pray, and read Quraan. This will allow your soul to feel more at ease before dozing off to sleep.

THERAPY

Although it's the first thing you should do after turning to Allaah, this is later on the list because if you are young, your parents are in charge of getting you into it.

Sometimes, it is not accessible for families to get, as therapy can be expensive, or some people may not believe it will really work. Always ask Allaah to make it easy for you to get the help you need. If you are constantly worried, scared, and paranoid to the point of physical symptoms, you should definitely get therapy, whether it be online or in person.

Therapists are trained to listen, care, and give solutions for problems we can't see our way out of. They can give you techniques to manage your problems and help you through what's making you anxious in the first place.

In the last few chapters, you learned about how to care for your soul and deal with all that's happening inside. This was so you could have the tools to keep yourself closely connected to Allaah and those you love, with a strong heart and mind that is peaceful and content.

However, there is more to being a Muslim than following the way of Islaam and having good character. You also have to avoid sins that will drag you down and hold you back from doing what's right and getting to Jannah.

There are many sins you'll have to avoid in life, since we are all naturally prone to falling into a few. As you grow, you'll learn about them more and more; the stronger your Imaan, the easier it will be to avoid them.

However, if you live in a Western, or non-Muslim country, there are many things that society widely practices and accepts which are completely Haraam for us. Certain things they do on the daily make your heart heavy and polluted and can lead you to the Hellfire, may Allaah protect us from that, Ameen.

There are three major normalized sins in the West that particularly affect you during the years of Puberty. They are common, expected behaviors for teens and early adults to partake in on a daily basis. These sins are easy for pre-teens to fall into because they appeal to their natural desire for emotional stimulation and experiences; a desire that is especially heightened during Puberty. In this chapter we will go over each of them in detail, Insha Allaah.

LISTENING TO MUSIC

One of the most common normalized sins is listening to music. In the West, music is a major part of the culture. You hear it in videos on social media, at the grocery store, on buses and trains, and even in the waiting room at the doctor's office.

Singers and musicians are praised and passionately followed by millions of people who will become aggressive with you for not liking their faves. Some artists from the West are incredibly popular, with their songs and videos being watched by millions or even billions of people! Music can also influence what people wear, the latest trends, and even the words we use. A lot of the slang, jokes, and phrases people say come from popular songs.

Almost since the beginning of time, music has been ingrained in culture, no matter what part of the world you are from. A common misconception is that music is Haraam because of bad lyrics, and that you can listen to music with clean lyrics, but that is not true. Although it is Haraam to listen to idle talk and singing that leads you to sinful and disbelieving acts, as said here in the Quraan:

> **"And of mankind is he who purchases Lahu Al-Hadeeth (music, singing) to mislead (men) from the path of Allaah without knowledge and takes it by way of mockery. For such there will be a humiliating torment." - [Quraan, 31:6]**

It is still not Halaal to listen to music, no matter how clean and uplifting the lyrics are. We have proof of that in the following Hadeeth.

> It was narrated Abu 'Amir or Abu Malik Al-Ash'ari that he heard the Prophet ﷺ saying: "From among my followers there will be some people who will consider illegal sexual intercourse, the wearing of silk, the drinking of alcoholic drinks and the use of musical instruments, as lawful..." - [al-Bukhaari]

The punishment for those who partake in these actions is mentioned at the end of the same Hadeeth:

> "...Allaah will destroy them during the night and will let the mountain fall on them, and He will transform the rest of them into monkeys and pigs and they will remain so till the Day of Resurrection." - [al-Bukhaari]

In many Western songs, the lyrics often have detailed descriptions of sex, drugs, crimes, and especially unlawful romantic relationships. This is followed by dances and music videos where the person singing is usually half naked, making sexual moves in the air or on the backup dancers, and starting dance challenges online where the average person can post themselves doing the same. It is impossible to separate music from zinaa, as no matter where you are in the world, music is always mostly about romance and sexual desires.

The danger of music is in its ability to change your mood, emotions, and spiritual energy. For the same reason we eat Halaal we must also avoid listening to music. If you fuel your body with things that are spiritually pure, you will live a better quality of life, and be able to worship with a clear heart and mind; If you fuel your body with useless, impure, and sinful things, you will feel heavy and sick inside, and your worship will suffer from a polluted mind, and blackening heart.

The right song can take you from mildly sad, to crying uncontrollably, from burning anger, to a chill mood, and from nonchalant, to a high of happiness. Music has the power to shift and sway your emotions, changing your energy, mood, and actions without you even realizing it.

As Muslims, we keep our energy pure, mood calm, and actions for the sake of Allaah. **By listening to music, you are allowing yourself to be controlled by a sin that can lead you to the Hellfire**, may Allaah protect us from that, ameen.

Listening to music on its own is sometimes easy for a person to avoid. But what about the music you listen to without thinking about it? Even when you're not trying to listen to music, it's everywhere, like in the background of videos on social media platforms such as TikTok, Instagram, and YouTube shorts. These videos are usually a popular clip of music in the background with a video playing based on the lyrics.

Without meaning to, you can click on any one of these apps and get sucked into them for hours on end. And when you're done, you will have listened to hours of music. Think of all the videos you may have clicked, liked, saved, or even posted to your own page, which will make the video more popular and give you bad deeds for helping others to listen to it.

Finally, dear reader, you must remember that your heart and mind soak things up like a sponge. It is easy to fill your mind with catchy lyrics and even remember them years after you have stopped listening to the song. If your mind is filled with music, memorizing the Quraan and being in the remembrance of Allaah becomes very difficult. It's like keeping a room clean—if you bring in things that don't belong, it's harder to make space for what truly matters. How many surahs can you recite off the top of your head without reviewing first?

How many times a day do ayaat pop into your mind, and you subconsciously recite along? Both are things music listeners experience daily. As a Muslim, you must always remember that your goal is to make it to Jannah. To accomplish this, you should always have Allaah in your thoughts as much as possible and get rid of habits that distract you from your faith.

UNLAWFUL TOUCH

It is only natural to hold hands, hug, and touch as you interact with your friends and family. However, when you become Mukallaf, there are two types of Haraam touch that you should know about.

The first is touching men in any way who aren't Mahram for you. In the ayah of hijaab, we learn who is Halaal for us to be uncovered and interact with, without the no touching rule. But anyone who is not included in this ayah is Haraam for us to touch in any way, such as shaking hands, hugging, normal touching, kissing, and anything else.

The people who are Halaal for us are our husbands, fathers, father-in-laws, sons, stepsons, brothers, nephews, other women, specific types of servants, and male children who haven't hit Puberty yet.

In the West, it is common to shake hands with new acquaintances, have male friends who casually touch and hug you, etc. But in Islaam, we understand that people connect through even casual touching and hugging, which can lead to inappropriate situations if people really like each other, or someone wants to take advantage of the other. To avoid this, men and women do not touch at all unless they are allowed for each other.

The second type of unlawful touch is when someone touches, rubs, or lingers on their own private parts to cause intimate feelings. This is called masturbation, which is Haraam in Islaam, and if it is done to the point where maniy (the discharge that comes from intimate touch) is released, you must take a ghusl as taught in part one before being able to pray again. This is because it is a minor version of the major sin, zinaa, and the punishment without true repentance and life changes is Hellfire. May Allaah prevent and protect us from entering Hellfire, Ameen.

Despite this, in the West, this behavior is encouraged and accepted as normal among children, young teens, and even adults. Sometimes, people do this because of their feelings when they see or think of deeply romantic scenarios. **The feeling is natural, but it is Haraam to act on without marriage, even if it is by your own hand.**

Saving intimate touch for marriage helps us build healthy and Halaal relationships that are sacred and special to us in this life, and help you get to Jannah in the next, Insha Allaah.

ADULT CONTENT

Although most people don't like to talk about this, adult content is an issue that affects children around the world, sometimes as young as six, with the average exposure being at eight years old. If you think this is a subject you can save for later, think again.

Because Muslim parents do not always speak to their children about subjects like these, they fall into it at an early age and become trapped with an addiction. Although this mostly affects boys, the amount of girls this is affecting is on the rise, and you must be sure to understand from the earliest age possible that this is not okay.

Adult content is videos, shows, clips, commercials, ads, or anything that shows people kissing, unlawfully, and intimately touching each other, especially when unclothed.

This type of content is called porn, and **just as it is Haraam to do these things in real life, it is also Haraam to watch others doing it through your screen.**

Even though it is referred to as Adult content in this chapter, that does not mean adults are allowed to see these things either. It is just as Haraam for them as it is for children, if not even more so, because they understand things that children do not and are being held accountable in the sight of Allaah.

If someone from school, your friend, or even a family member tries to show you this content, understand that it is Haraam, inappropriate, and a form of sexual abuse. You must tell them to stop, run away, and tell a trusted adult immediately!

Even if it is animated as a cartoon, in anime style, or a drawing or fan art of your favorite characters from the show you like, if they are unclothed, kissing, unlawfully, or intimately touching other characters or themselves, this is still Haraam, adult content!

Young children can quickly become addicted to this content because the chemicals and feelings it releases in the brain are similar to those that are released in drug addicts. That is why you must learn that it is Haraam as early as possible because addiction is hard to get rid of and something that may follow you well into adulthood.

For some, it becomes a lifelong struggle to keep away from, and negatively affects their lives, Imaan, and marriages for years on end.

In the West, minor forms of adult content, such as being half-clothed while kissing or inappropriately dancing or touching, can come at you from any angle. Sometimes even billboards on the highway, posters at the mall or in stores, commercials, ads on websites, and between videos, movies, and shows can all feature adult content. Music videos and dance challenges are especially notorious for this, and so are social media platforms such as YouTube, Instagram, TikTok, and especially Twitter. Even children's shows and movies are beginning to feature minor forms of adult content more and more.

These are also things we must stay away from since they lead to the worst forms of adult content mentioned above. Here is what Islaam says about this kind of content in the Quraan and Hadeeth:

> "Tell the believing men to lower their gaze (from looking at forbidden things), And protect their private parts (from illegal sexual Acts). That is pure for them. Verily Allaah is All aware of what they do." - [Quraan, 24:30]

Here we see that Allaah is telling the believers to lower their gazes, meaning to protect their eyes from seeing Haraam things and to guard their private parts. Allaah also reminds us that He is always watching and knows everything we are doing at all times.

> Abu Huraira narrated that the Messenger of Allaah ﷺ said: "Allaah fixed the very portion of adultery which a man will indulge in. There would be no escape from it. The adultery of the eye is the lustful look and the adultery of the ears is listening to voluptuous (song or talk) and the adultery of the tongue is licentious speech and the adultery of the hand is the lustful grip (embrace) and the adultery of the feet is to walk (to the place) where he intends to commit adultery and the heart yearns and desires which he may or may not put into effect." - [Sahih Muslim]

From this Hadeeth, we can see that what we watch, listen to, and how we touch all contribute to unlawful touch, and we must be careful to stay away from the things that may cause us to commit major sins.

Finally, the effects of watching adult content are very bad for your mind and soul. Being exposed to such behavior on this level harms the way you look at others and how you approach life. **It causes the watchers to become perverted and more likely to intimately and unlawfully touch others and themselves.**

When you watch things that give you a rush, like inappropriate content, certain chemicals in your brain such as serotonin, dopamine, and norepinephrine increase. These chemicals help control how you feel, move, digest food, and what makes you feel happy. If these chemicals are too heightened, it will imbalance your brain, making you always want to go back to whatever made them spike. This happens especially during Puberty, a time when you're naturally wired to seek out new experiences and emotions. That is how your brain changes when you have an addiction to adult content. **Not only does it mess with your brain's natural balance, but it can also lead to other symptoms, such as:**

✦ Heavy guilt and shame
✦ Withdrawing from friends and family
✦ Depression and anxiety
✦ Not being able to become happy or excited easily
✦ Uncontrollable bad language and perverted thinking
✦ Low self-worth
✦ Strong urges to unlawfully touch yourself and others
✦ Believing you will never be forgiven, and stuck this way forever
✦ Abandoning spiritual needs such as prayer, Duaa, Quraan, and properly covering
✦ Losing faith in Allaah

If someone finds themselves struggling with an addiction to this, the only way to stop is by turning to Allaah, asking forgiveness and freedom from this addiction, and getting professional therapy. They must make real life changes, such as eliminating the loneliness, depression, or stress that is causing them to turn to this. They should take preventative steps like staying offline, putting restrictions on their devices, and replacing their brain's need for the chemical rises with something else that is Halaal and suits them. For some, it is vigorous exercise, taking time to memorize the Quraan, or pursuing a mentally engaging job or hobby. It is a hard process that takes dedication and time to work, but in the end, it's worth it for this life and the next.

If you have come across adult content, make sure to ask Allaah's forgiveness, ask him to keep it away from you, and never go back to it again. Parents can also put restrictions on your devices to make sure you are not exposed to inappropriate content. May Allaah protect us from the dangers of adult content, Ameen.

It is only natural to touch as you interact with people during your everyday life, but some places on your body, dear reader, are completely off-limits. Not just for friends and strangers but also for your family. As you grow into a young woman, it is important to know what touch is safe and normal vs. unsafe and abusive. Your body has boundaries that others are never allowed to cross, and knowing what they are is crucial for your physical, mental, and spiritual health and safety.

Safe touch is between friends and family, such as light touches when playing a game, arm wrestling, playing patty cake, holding hands, having an arm over someone's shoulder, hugging, kissing on the cheek, and sitting close together on the couch. **Both of you are okay with the interaction, and it is all in lighthearted fun, or showing someone you care.**

Unsafe touch is when the touch is done out of lust to someone who does not want it, and is Haraam to be doing it with at all. If someone touches, rubs, or lingers their hands or private parts on places of your body that are off limits, **this is unsafe touch and a type of sexual abuse called molestation.** This kind of abuse can happen to anyone—adults, children, boys or girls.

Places you may be uncomfortable with others touching:

+ Your neck and shoulders
+ Your stomach
+ Your upper thighs
+ Your legs and feet

Places that are off-limits to others both on top and under your clothes:

+ Your chest
+ Your vagina (private area), between your legs, and your butt.
+ Touching their lips to your lips

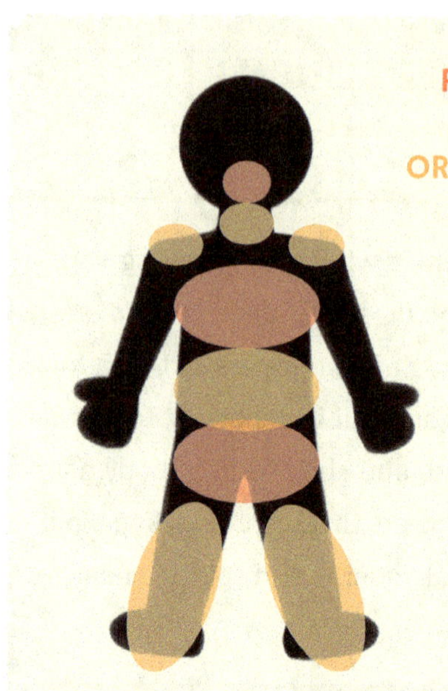

It's not only unsafe and abuse if someone touches, lingers, or rubs you in your unsafe areas, but it is also unsafe and abuse for you to do this to others, and for them to tell you to touch them in their unsafe places.

Never believe anyone who tries to convince you that this is okay. In Islaam, it is Haraam to touch, linger, and sexually rub your own private parts, or anyone else's unless you are married to them. This is a sin that will lead people to Hellfire and to get tormented in their graves, especially if they are abusing someone while doing it. May Allaah prevent and protect us all from this, Ameen.

Even outside of Islaam, this behavior is completely unacceptable and illegal. When caught, people who sexually abuse others will go to jail. Unfortunately, some people who abuse this way don't go to jail because the child or adult they've abused is too scared to tell on them. This is because they use other kinds of abusive methods to make their victims keep it a secret.

The only time people are allowed to see your private areas or touch them is if, for example, the doctor has to check on you. This, too, should only happen with your parents' permission. When you're older, you are allowed to refuse this part of the check-up due to your religion if you are uncomfortable with it.

Another time this may be okay is if a parent or nurse needs to help you with bathing or wiping. At your age, you can likely do this on your own, but this can still apply if you've had an injury or disability that prevents you from doing this yourself.

WHO ARE SEXUAL ABUSERS?

Know that you must always ask Allaah to protect you against this, and in general, AlHamdulillaah, most families care about and protect each other. However, in 90% of the cases of child molestation, it is someone close to or in the family who does this to them. That doesn't mean it will happen to you. May Allaah protect you from this, Ameen. But for people it does happen to; unfortunately, this is the reality.

Sometimes, it's an uncle, aunt, grandfather, babysitter, mother or father figure, a parent's friend, or, in rare and unfortunate cases, even a parent. Sometimes, it's not an adult but a child your age or another young person; it can even be a sibling or a cousin.

Besides people you know, it can also be a neighbor or a stranger, which is why you must stay close to your family when you're outside and avoid being alone with anyone you don't know or are uncomfortable with.

Remember that even if the person who does this is a respected person in your family, they are still a sexual abuser whom Allaah will punish and who should be put in prison. People who do this usually abuse not only one person but multiple people and try to keep it a secret.

These people can be from forums and chats, social media, or anywhere else where people can interact online. Once again, sometimes it's not an adult; it can be a child your age or another young person. For this reason, avoid chatting with strangers online and use social media for what it was intended for, which is keeping in touch with friends and family.

Once again, may Allaah protect us all from this and save those who are suffering and have suffered from it, Ameen.

HOW DO ABUSERS KEEP IT A SECRET?

Sexual abusers are cowards and scummy human beings, to say the least. They abuse children or others and always try to keep it a secret. To do this, they manipulate the person they abuse by using threats, lies, and fear to stop them from telling others and getting help.

HERE ARE THE TACTICS ABUSERS USE:

THREATEN - Saying they will hurt the child, their family, or others they care about if they don't keep it a secret.

LOVE - Sometimes, the abuser will try to give the child gifts or be their friend to make the child have a crush on them or love them. This can make the victim feel like the abuse is okay or not even abuse in the first place. It can make them not want to get the person in trouble or not tell because they feel like they will lose the person they like.

FEAR - Sometimes, an abuser will say things like, "No one will believe you, no one will care, and nothing will happen if you tell." This also goes back to threatening, where they say they will hurt them or someone they love or care about.

BLAME - Some abusers will tell the person they are abusing that it's their fault for dressing a certain way, looking good to them, being friendly or flirting with them, or saying they were bad, so they have to punish them. All of these things are NEVER an excuse for unsafe touching.

SHAME - Because it is their private area, some people are too embarrassed to tell that this has happened to them. Sexual abuse leaves a person feeling dirty, ashamed, and like they aren't worth getting help. Remember, the person this happens to is NOT dirty; the person who did it to them, is.

The only one who should be ashamed is the abuser. We are the creation of Allaah, and our bodies were given to us by Him to take care of while we are on earth. Sometimes, you can't protect yourself, and that's not your fault at all. Just know that you should do your duty as a Muslim and get help for abuse that is happening to your body by telling someone immediately.

GETTING IN TROUBLE - Sometimes, a child or older person will think that no one will believe them, that it was their fault, or that the adult they tell won't understand them and will get them in trouble. None of these are ever true.

GASLIGHTING - If the person they have abused tries to tell them it was wrong and to stop, abusers often try to make it seem like what they did was not a big deal or anything to worry about to make the victim feel like they are overreacting and crazy for feeling angry, sad, or distressed because of the abuse.

GROOMING - Grooming is when a sexual abuser builds a relationship with a child or adult so they can easily abuse them. This goes back to the love tactic, except someone who is groomed sometimes does not like the person but accepts the abuse because they are used to them and have been convinced that it's okay.

This can happen by the abuser giving the person gifts or making them rely on them for love and support. Gifts and closeness to others aren't bad by themselves as long as they aren't inappropriate, but they take it further by making the victim think they love them while convincing them that their unsafe touches are okay because they're out of love or care.

WHAT SHOULD BE DONE?

Again, may Allaah prevent and protect us from this and save and have mercy on those who have suffered from this or are still suffering from this, Ameen. However, if you find yourself in a situation where you feel unsafe touch will happen, or it has been happening to you, below are the things you can do to get away from it or stop it from happening again.

Keep in mind that when a situation like this happens, your body can go into survival mode, which means your brain might be too freaked out to think of the list you read here. Instead, it might freeze or disassociate (the mind drifting out of reality) because the situation is too much to handle. That is why most of the things on the list are things to do afterward, as you never know how your body will react to abuse.

+ Know that the person doing it is a sexual Abuser and deserves to be punished.
+ Scream and yell.
+ Bite as hard as you can.

- ✦ Run immediately.
- ✦ Tell Immediately (a parent, teacher, trusted family/adult, or police)
- ✦ Keep close to your family in public, don't be willingly alone
- ✦ Have a secret code with your parents or trusted caregiver that you can text or call and say that will let them know you are in trouble, need to be picked up, or something dangerous is going on.
- ✦ Always say the morning and evening Duaa's, and pray to Allaah to protect you and others from this.
- ✦ Understand that none of this was your fault, and it is up to your parents and caretakers to make sure this never happens again.

Police (in the USA) are required by law to immediately detain a sexual abuser and check on the victim to get them the help they need. If you are ever afraid to go to an adult you know, call the police. If you are scared to go to the police yourself, **tell a teacher, who is required by law (in the USA) to call the police immediately.** If the US laws don't apply to you, find out your regions procedure for sexual abuse online.

HOW CAN SOMEONE HEAL FROM THIS?

STEP ONE - GETTING AWAY FROM THE ABUSE

You cannot heal from something that is still happening to you. The abuser must be punished and separated from the victim for good. Then, if possible, the person who has been harmed should leave or never return to the environment where the abuse took place. Whether it be a school, a family member's house, a room in their own home, or a neighborhood that leaves them vulnerable to more abuse and physical reminders of what happened to them.

STEP TWO - PROFESSIONAL HELP

Sexual abuse changes the way a person thinks and feels about the world, and especially themselves. It can leave long-lasting bad memories, fear, sadness, and turmoil in someone's life. Without the help of someone who cares, a victim of this abuse can turn to coping in ways that damage their life even further.

After having the support of loving family and friends who will protect, listen, and help them heal, a person who has been sexually abused should get professional help if possible. A Therapist is a doctor for your heart and mind, and if you are hurting inside, they are trained to help you heal with techniques and wisdom that an untrained person may not be able to give you.

STEP THREE - SPIRITUAL HEALING

Allaah gave us so much more than just rules in the way of Islaam. He also gave us healing, wisdom, love, and mercy. He knows us more than we can ever know ourselves. He is always watching and loves us even more than our wonderful mothers who gave birth to us. When no human can understand you and feel what you feel, Allaah is there. He knows, He cares, He will protect you and free you from what is harming you. If no one on earth is in your corner, know that Allaah is, and the closer you get to Him, the more He will make things right in your life and heal what has been broken in your heart and soul.

Part Three
BEAUTY & STYLE

HAIR-TYPE HAIR-CARE

You can tell so much about a person by how they keep their hair. Your hair can be a sign of who you are and where you come from. The way you style it says a lot about your personality and can completely make or break your look. If your hair is messy, you look messy. If your hair is beautifully done, you look beautiful and well put together.

If you allow your hair to be tangled constantly, have an odor, and look like you just rolled out of bed, others might make negative comments about it or see you as an unkempt or lazy person. This perception from others, along with your own feelings about your undone hair can affect your self-image and cause low self-esteem and confidence. Think of your hair as a part of you that deserves care and attention, after all, it's a representation of who you are. You must have pride in the way you care for and style it. If your hair is done, not only do you look good, but feel good, too. Take your hair care seriously, dear reader, and see how much better your self-confidence will become, Insha Allaah.

This is easier said than done of course, since it sometimes takes a while to learn to love your natural hair or know how to care for it best. Perhaps you feel that your hair is too unruly or not as you'd like, so you neglect it or do extreme treatments to change it. There is also the matter of finding hairstyles that will look good on you and are simple enough to keep up with and do on your own. A part of growing up is taking care of yourself both inside and out. It might seem tough at first, but with a bit of practice, you'll find that hair care is a lot easier and more rewarding than you first thought.

HAIR IN ISLAAM

In Islaam, hair care is very important because a Muslim must always look clean and presentable, especially for worship. Although Muslim women do not show their hair in public, this does not mean you don't have to take care of it or put in any less work to keep it looking nice.

> **Abu Hurairah narrated that the Prophet ﷺ said: "Whoever has hair should look after it." - [Abu Dawood]**

In this Hadeeth, we can see that when combing his hair, the Prophet ﷺ would start from the right side.

> **Aisha ﷺ narrated that: "The Prophet ﷺ liked Tayammun (starting with the right side) when putting on his shoes, combing his hair, performing wudhoo and bathing, and in all his affairs." - [al-Bukhaari]**

Another Sunnah is dyeing the hair with Henna.

> **Abu Huraira ﷺ narrated that the Prophet ﷺ said: "The Jews and the Christians do not dye their hair, so be different from them." - [al-Bukhaari]**

The Prophet ﷺ took care of his hair by combing and oiling it, a practice that his wife Aisha ﷺ was reported to do for him often.

> **Aisha ﷺ narrated: "While in menses, I used to comb the hair of Allaah's Messenger ﷺ." - [al-Bukhaari]**

> Aisha ﷺ narrated that: "Allaah's Messenger ﷺ used to let his head in (the house) while he was in the masjid and I would comb and oil his hair. When in I`tikaf he used not to enter the house except for a need." - [al-Bukhaari]

Human hair is to be cherished in Islaam, especially a woman's hair. This is why even though men shave their heads for Umrah and Hajj, women only have to cut a small amount of theirs.

> Ibn Abbaas ﷺ narrated that the Messenger of Allaah ﷺ said: "Women (pilgrims) do not have to shave (their heads); they may only shorten their hair." - [Abu Dawood]

As a Muslim, ghusls will be something you have to do often, which includes washing your hair, specifically your scalp. Depending on how often you must take a ghusl, the extra washing could dry out your hair. That's why knowing how to take care of it is so important.

In caring for the wonderful body Allaah has given you, you must keep your hair healthy and strong as a part of being thankful to Him.

HOW DO I WASH MY HAIR?

Before getting into the twelve hair types, and finding out which one is yours, here is a simple hair wash routine that will work for almost everyone, and be easy to maintain. **Depending on your hair type, you can add or take away steps, as well as choose the products that are right for you.**

WHAT WATER TEMPERATURE IS BEST?

COLD WATER is good for hair growth because it improves blood circulation; it also closes the pores of your scalp, which will lock in your hair moisture and give it an extra shine. If you have an oily scalp, you might not want to use cold water, since it locks in that extra oil.

LUKEWARM WATER gives your hair a gentle, cleansing wash while opening up the hair follicles just enough to let a good amount of product into your scalp.

HOT WATER makes it easier to wash out dirt and grime, but also strips your hair of its natural oils. If you have an extra oily scalp, this may not be a bad thing, however, hot water also opens up your pores and dries the scalp, as well as weakens your hair strands. If you have a dry scalp, hot water is a big no-no.

HAIR WASH ROUTINE

1. DETANGLE AND RINSE
2. SHAMPOO
3. CONDITION
4. DETANGLE WHILE DAMP

STEP ONE - DETANGLE AND RINSE

Before adding product, make sure your hair is completely soaked with water. This will help activate the products you use and make it easier for them to lather and reach all of your hair strands. However, if you have curly or coily hair that tends to tangle, brush or comb your hair gently while damp (slightly wet, not soaking) before getting it fully soaked. This will allow you to shed less hair and form fewer tangles as you shampoo.

Shampoo is a product used to clean your hair. Place a reasonable amount on your palm based on how much hair you have, and gently work it into your scalp using the pads of your fingertips (not your nails) with back-and-forth hand motions, since circular motions will tangle your hair. You can also use a silicone scalp massager to spread the shampoo. Keep in mind that you should be gentle while doing this, since harshly rubbing your scalp is not necessary and can do more harm than good.

Only apply the shampoo to your scalp, and don't rub it into the rest of your hair. When your hair is wet, it is weak, and the extra rubbing can cause your hair to break. Instead, focus on cleaning your scalp, which is where your hair is most healthy and strong. **Let the shampoo clean the rest by gently lathering it a few times and letting it run down your hair.** Avoid rubbing the shampoo into the ends of your hair, especially since that is where it is least healthy and is coming to the end of its life. This will just cause it to break off, and the extra friction will only make it weaker.

Remember not to use an excessive amount of shampoo. As long as your hair is covered in the product, that is enough. Adding too much will only give you extra suds, which doesn't actually mean your hair is getting any cleaner and will just be a waste of product.

After thoroughly washing your scalp and allowing the shampoo to cleanse the rest of your hair, rinse all the shampoo out until the water runs clear. You can also wash it until your hair squeaks when you rub it between your fingers, but keep in mind that could be a sign that you stripped your hair of its natural oils, and it should only be done if your hair is extra oily.

Depending on your hair type, or how much build up was in it, you may have to shampoo two to three more times before your hair is completely clean.

If you usually have a lot of dandruff, use a dandruff shampoo. If your hair is extra oily, use a lightweight shampoo that isn't made with lots of oils. If your hair is dry, use an extra moisturizing shampoo with heavy oils in it.

Avoid shampoos with ingredients like **Parabens** (a chemical that disrupts your hormones), **Silicones** (an ingredient that coats your hair, preventing moisture), **Sulfates** (an ingredient that over cleanses and dries out your hair), and **Formaldehyde** (a chemical that can be cancerous and cause irritation or rashes to the skin in some cases). In general, try to get chemical-free shampoos from brands that use natural ingredients.

STEP THREE - CONDITION

Conditioner is a product that moisturizes, softens, and gives a glimmering shine to your hair. Place a reasonable amount in your palm based on how much hair you have, and using your fingers or a comb to run it through evenly, apply it to your hair strands and ends, not your scalp. The scalp creates its own moisture, and especially if you have oily hair, you do not want to over-moisturize. Your hair strands and ends are what need conditioner to stay strong since it doesn't get as much oil as the top of the hair, and the ends are close to dying off. Leave the conditioner in your hair for around a minute or so before washing it out.

If your hair is harder to detangle, leave the conditioner in for detangling, and do not wash it out. If your hair is dry, use a heavy conditioner that is extra moisturizing with nourishing oils in it. If your hair is oily, use a light conditioner that won't overpower your hair with extra oils.

STEP FOUR - DETANGLE WHILE DAMP

Allow your hair to slightly dry before detangling. If you try to brush your hair out while it is sopping wet, it will easily break off and make it harder to get the knots out. To do this, you can let it partially air dry, or use a towel to get rid of the excess water. You should use a microfiber towel or a cotton T-shirt for this part since regular towels can cause frizz and breakage on freshly wet hair by being too harsh.

When your hair is damp, it is the best time to detangle. If your hair is curly or coily, finger detangle as much as possible before using a brush or comb. This will allow less shedding and get the bigger tangles out easier. Next, use a comb or brush that works well for your hair type (which you will learn about later in this chapter, Insha Allaah), and **gently detangle from the ends of your hair to the top, always brushing or combing downward, not up, or to the side.** Depending on your hair type, you may need to do this in sections and add extra oils or detangler to make the process easier for you.

The rest of your hair routine, such as drying, oiling, and styling, will all depend on the type of hair you have. However, no matter which one it is, allow your hair to dry before styling it.

If you style your hair while wet, you may find that it takes on a musty smell later in the day from the bacteria, fungi, and dirt that may have built up in it. Either keep your hair out to let it naturally dry over the next few hours or blow dry it.

You cannot blow dry your hair while it is sopping wet. You must wait for it to be damp after wearing a towel or allowing it to air dry a little. Although you can do it if safely done, it is better not to use heat on your hair, as it can damage it, making it break off, stop growing, or become dry and brittle.

THE TWELVE HAIR TYPES

Just as Allaah created us in all different shapes, sizes, tribes, and colors, He has also given us different kinds of hair. The best way to care for your hair is to get to know it first. Knowing your hair type is essential to understanding how to properly care for it. Your hair type is what tells you what products to buy, what routine you should have, how to tie your hair up at night, and how you style it.

Sometimes you might see photos of hairstyles and get frustrated when they don't turn out the same on your own hair. That is because there are different types of hair, and one girl's style or hair routine may not work for you or even ruin your hair if you tried it.

There are four overall types of hair, they are straight, wavy, curly, and coily. Within each one, there is a range of three types, which are separated by letters A, B, and C. Sometimes you can have a mix of similar hair types on different parts of your head.

The best way to know your natural hair type is by looking at it when it's completely dry and untouched by a straightener, curler, perm, relaxer, or heavy products weighing it down. Each of these hair patterns has its own strengths and do's and don'ts. As long as you follow them, your hair should stay healthy, strong, and beautiful, Insha Allaah.

TYPE ONE - STRAIGHT HAIR

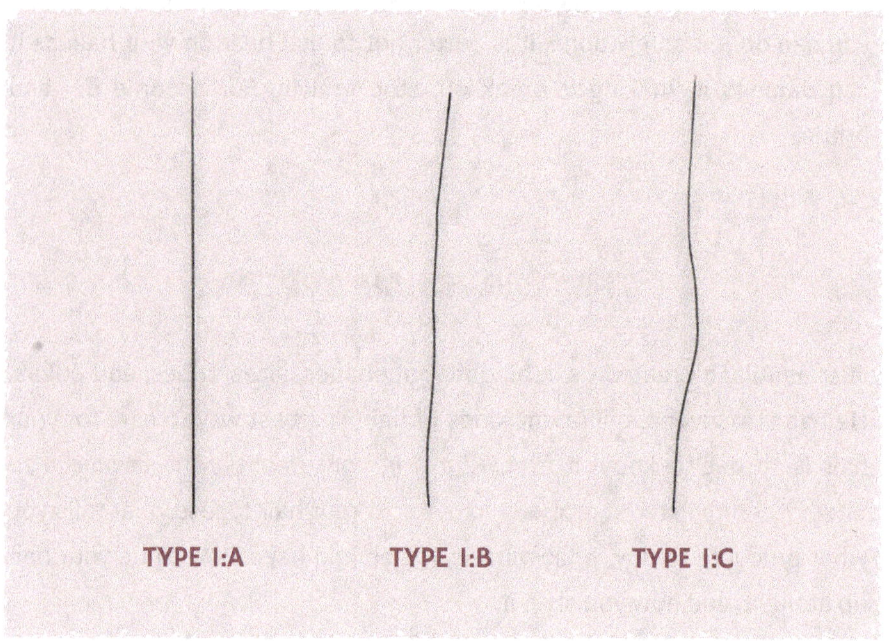

TYPE 1:A is straight with no curl or wave in sight. It is usually silky but thin and easily becomes oily.

TYPE 1:B is straight and thicker than 1:A, can have a hint of a wave, and easily becomes tangled and oily.

TYPE 1:C is straight, thick, and full, with slight bends in the hair; it can easily become frizzy and oily.

Straight hair should be washed every other day or at least twice a week so it doesn't become oily, weighed down, or stuck to your head. Use products that are light and won't cause a lot of oil buildup.

Use a paddle brush to detangle and a soft boar bristle brush to style this hair type. If you want your hair not to look flat on your scalp, use a round brush to create volume.

After washing this hair type, use a microfiber towel or T-shirt to dry your hair instead of a harsh towel. Allow it to air dry, or use a dryer on a cool setting to avoid heat damage. **Do not carelessly blow your hair around when drying**; instead, use a comb or brush to guide the hair downward while following that direction with the dryer. You can also use a dryer that already has a brush attached; this will allow the hair to dry neatly and tangle-free.

When fully dry, apply a small amount of light oils such as olive, argon, almond, rosemary, or jojoba oil to your scalp.

Many pretty styles can be done with straight hair. You can leave it out, put it in a ponytail, pigtails, half up, half down, a slicked back bun, a cute classic braid, french braids, fishtail braids, and much more!

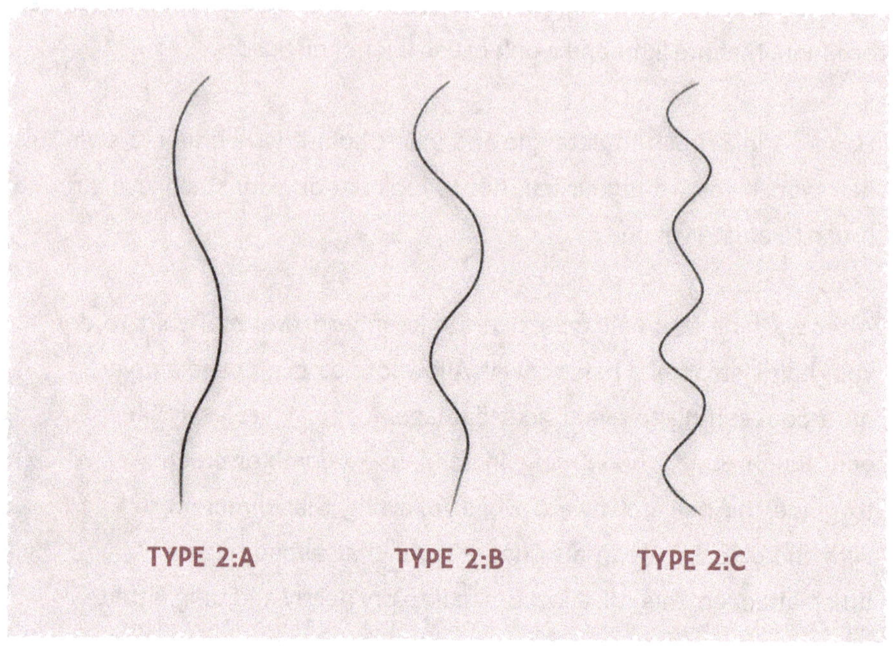

TYPE 2:A is straight at the root with light, loose waves, and easily becomes oily.

TYPE 2:B is a loose S-shaped wave, and is usually thinner and less oily than type 2:A. It can be easily flattened by heavy products.

TYPE 2:C is a tight S-shaped wave that starts close to the root and can easily become frizzy and dry.

Wavy hair should be washed once or twice a week to get rid of extra oil and dirt. This hair type should be moisturized with a leave-in conditioner or a hair mask. Light oils are good for your scalp, but avoid heavy butters and creams that weigh the hair down or give it an oily buildup. Use a vented paddle, or Denman brush to detangle, and a boar bristle brush to help style wavy hair.

After washing this hair type, use a microfiber towel or T-shirt to dry your hair instead of a harsh towel. Allow it to air dry, or use a dryer on a cool setting to avoid heat damage. **Do not carelessly blow your hair around when drying, especially if you want your waves to shine.** You can either brush and dry downwards like the last hair type or define your waves.

WAVY HAIR ROUTINE

1. Detangle while damp
2. Apply a light curl cream or hair mousse
3. Twist waves around your finger or hairbrush handle
4. Apply a lightweight gel by scrunching upwards from the ends
5. Allow to air dry or use a diffuser (a hair dryer attachment that evenly spreads the air throughout your hair)
6. Apply a light oil for moisture

When fully dry, apply a small amount of light oils such as olive, argon, coconut, rosemary, almond, or jojoba oil to the scalp and hair strands.

Many pretty styles can be done with wavy hair You can leave it out, put it in a ponytail, pigtails, half up, half down, a slicked back bun, a cute classic braid, french braids, fishtail braids, and much more!

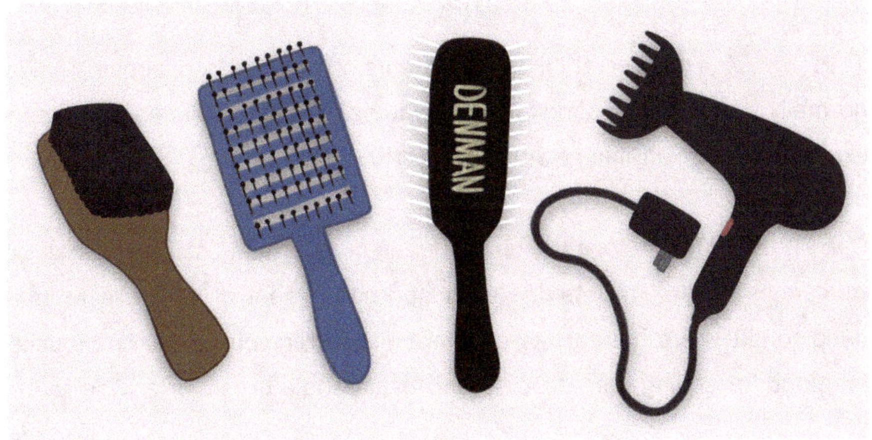

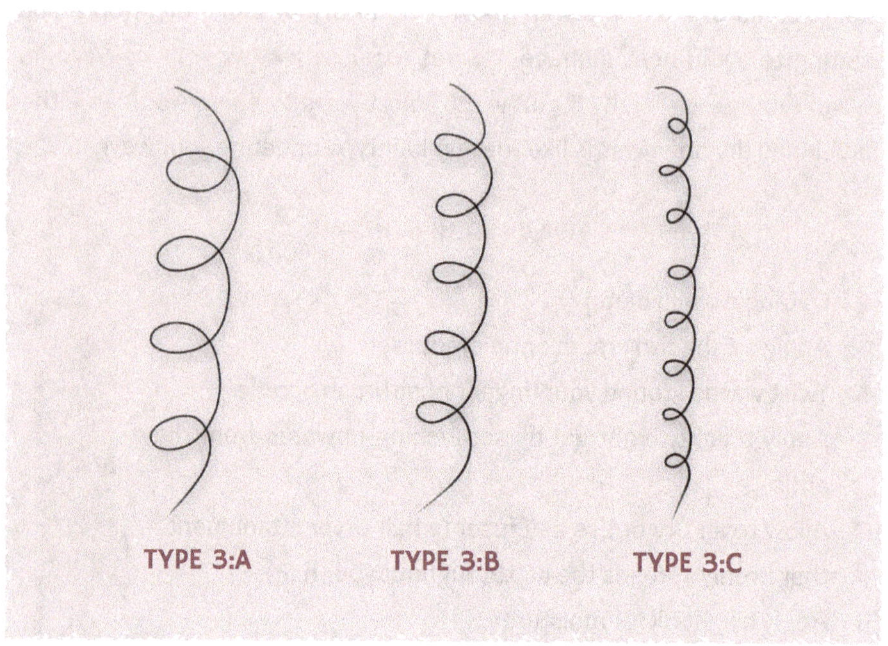

TYPE 3:A is thick, bouncy ringlets that are usually well-defined and can be easily weighed down by too much product. These curls are normally as wide as sidewalk chalk.

TYPE 3:B has a tighter curl than type 3:A and is normally in ringlets as wide as your pointer finger. This hair type can easily experience shrinkage and dryness.

TYPE 3:C is a tighter, thicker curl than both mentioned above and is normally in ringlets or corkscrews as wide as a pencil. This hair type can experience more shrinkage and dryness than the others.

Curly hair should be washed once a week or so and moisturized three or four times a week. It gets dry easily and needs a lot of moisture, so use deep conditioners, hair masks, and light oils. Curling custards and mousse are good for styling. Use a Denman brush, paddle brush, or a wide-tooth comb to detangle, and a boar bristle brush for styling. After washing this hair type, use a microfiber towel or T-shirt to dry your hair instead of a harsh towel. Allow it to air dry, or use a dryer on a cool setting to avoid heat damage. **Do not carelessly blow your hair around when drying, especially if you want your curls to shine.** You can either brush and dry in a downward direction or define your curls.

CURLY HAIR ROUTINE

1. Detangle while damp
2. Apply a light curl cream or hair mousse
3. Twist curls around your finger
4. Apply a lightweight gel by scrunching upwards from the ends
5. Allow to air dry or use a diffuser by lifting the ends of your hair gently up to your head
6. Apply a light oil for moisture

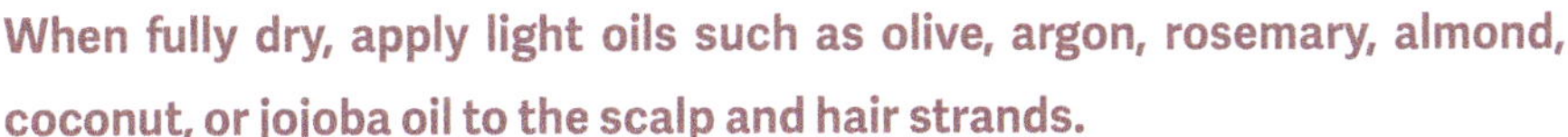

When fully dry, apply light oils such as olive, argon, rosemary, almond, coconut, or jojoba oil to the scalp and hair strands.

Many pretty styles can be done with curly hair. You can leave it out, put it in a ponytail, pigtails, half up, half down, a slicked back bun, a cute classic braid, french braids, flat twists, cornrows, box braids, twists, and more!

164

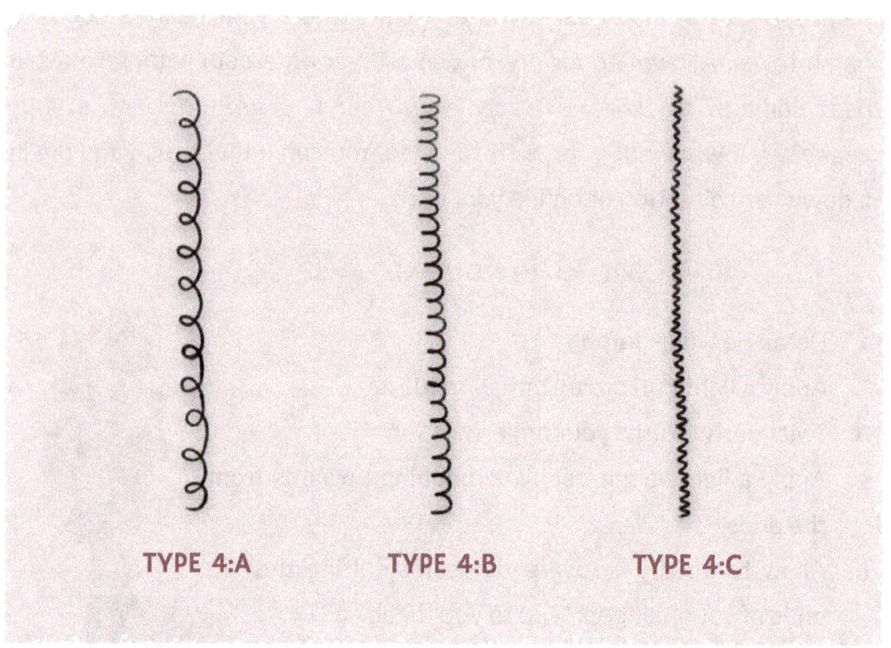

TYPE 4:A is springy, thick, and full coils that are slimmer than the last type. This hair type is prone to dryness and needs lots of moisture.

TYPE 4:B is tight, thick, zigzag coils that are full and intertwined and give a puffy appearance. This hair type is prone to high levels of shrinkage and needs lots of moisture.

TYPE 4:C is thick, kinky coils that are heavily intertwined and dense and give the wearer a nice fro. This hair type experiences the highest level of shrinkage and needs the most moisture.

Coily hair should be washed between once a week to once a month, and should be moisturized with a leave-in conditioner and heavy oils every day.

You should be gentle when styling coily hair since it is prone to breakage. Always pay attention to your scalp, and make sure to apply oil there especially. A healthy scalp means a healthy head of hair. Use a Denman brush, paddle brush, hair pick, or a wide-tooth comb to detangle, and a boar bristle brush for styling.

Detangling should be done in sections with lots of leave-in conditioner, always finger detangle before using a brush or comb to do the rest. If your hair is braided, in plaits, or in cornrows, you can wash it as normal; just be sure to use leave-in conditioner and good-smelling oils and allow it to fully dry to avoid an unpleasant damp odor.

How you choose to dry your hair depends on how you plan to style it. If you are planning to braid, straighten, or slick your hair into a bun or ponytail, you can brush and blow-dry it in a downward direction to stretch it for styling. **It's best to use an all-in-one volumizing hair dryer brush to do so.** This way, you won't have to juggle both a brush and dryer while trying to stretch your hair.

if you wish to leave it out and have curls, you can do a braid/twist out. But If you want to define your coils, then while your hair is damp, simply add a curl custard and/or hair mousse and/or hair gel and evenly distribute the product throughout your hair. Allow it to air dry, and your coils will be bouncy, shiny, and beautiful.

HOW TO DO A BRAID/TWIST OUT

1. Detangle while damp
2. Heavily moisturize
3. Braid/twist hair to desired curl size
4. Allow to air dry
5. Undo braids/twists
6. Separate curls with your fingers

You can also do so many pretty braided and twisted styles with coily hair. Box braids, cornrows, twists, and flat twists will keep your hair styled for three weeks to a month or more while being a protective style that allows it to grow. This is also ideal for a Muslim woman who must have her hair pulled back or styled flatly under her hijaab and may need to take ghusls often, which is easier to do if the hair is braided since you won't have to detangle it.

No matter how you decide to style your hair, **keep your scalp and strands moisturized with heavy oils such as shea, mango, or cocoa butter, and castor oil. Once a month, a hot oil treatment is beneficial.**

FOR ALL HAIR TYPES

If you need hairstyle inspiration, look online for your type hairstyles and save the ones you like. If there is a style you don't know how to do, follow a tutorial and practice until you've perfected it. Try to find one that is simple enough for you to do every day or once a week; and for type 3 and 4, ones that you can do once or twice a month and won't have to take out for three to four weeks. Make sure it suits your style, and **keep in mind offering wudhoo, taking a ghusl, and wearing hijaab when choosing your go-to hairstyle.**

Sleeping with a satin pillowcase is best, especially for types 3 and 4, where a satin scarf or bonnet is needed for keeping your hair frizz and tangle-free throughout the night. This will also preserve your hairstyle, making it last longer and still be neat after a night of tossing and turning. Other materials might cause your hair to tangle, frizz, and dry out.

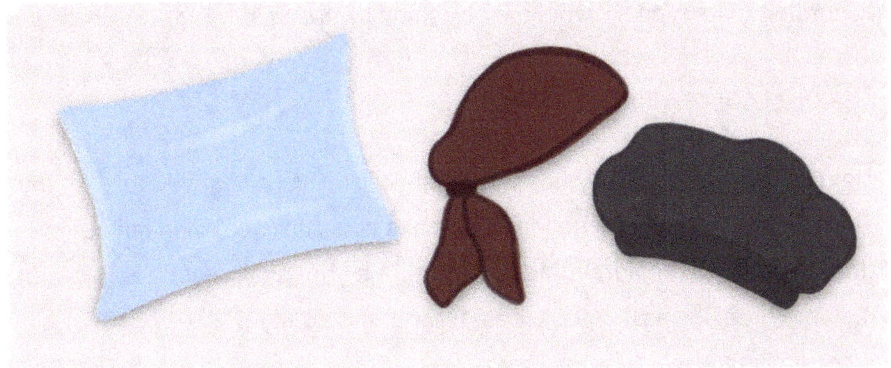

WHAT CAUSES HAIR DAMAGE?

OVERHEATING

Using straighteners, curlers and high-heat dryers can damage your hair severely. Heat-damaged hair is always dry and brittle, no matter how much oil you add to it. It easily falls out, always looks frizzy and dead, and will severely slow down hair growth and ruin your curl pattern if you have one. Heat-damaged hair is better to be trimmed off little by little as your new, healthy hair grows in. **To avoid overheating, try not to use hot hair tools at all, but if you must, use a generous amount of heat protectant, set the tool to medium or low heat, and don't do too many passes through the same section.**

Until you're old enough to properly understand how to do it yourself, it's best to go to a trusted adult who knows what they're doing to safely use the hot hair tool for you.

OVER WASHING

Over washing your hair can dry it out, making it brittle, frizzy, prone to breakage, and slow down your hair growth. This is why it is important to know your hair type and follow a wash routine accordingly. If you must take ghusls often, be sure to give extra moisture and care to your hair according to its type to avoid over washing symptoms.

TIGHT STYLES

Tight buns, braids, or any hairstyle that pulls at your scalp is not healthy. This can give you severe headaches, make your hair weak and fall out over time, and cause tension bumps to appear on your scalp. **Avoid this by not making your hair too tight when styling or harshly pulling at the scalp when detangling.**

HARSH CHEMICALS

Coloring, relaxing, and perming your hair can all be done safely with the right tools and professionals doing the work. However, **you should never perm, relax, or bleach your hair on your own until you are old enough not to need adult supervision.** Even coloring with box dye can lead to mishaps if done incorrectly. Over-perming, relaxing, bleaching, or coloring your hair can lead to it falling out in clumps, becoming dry and brittle, ruining your hair texture and curl pattern if you have one, and always having a frizzy and dead appearance. Besides harsh hair-changing chemicals, chemicals in shampoo, conditioner, and other hair products could be ruining your hair and stopping its growth without you knowing. **Sulfates** (which strip natural oils and dry hair), **alcohol** (which dries hair and promotes hair loss), **fragrance** (which irritates the scalp), and **parabens** (which irritate and dry your scalp, and can cause hair loss) are all bad ingredients to avoid when choosing products.

WHAT IS HARAAM TO DO WITH MY HAIR?

SHAVING YOURSELF BALD

In Islaam, it is okay for a woman to cut her hair, as we must do this during Hajj and Umrah, and the Prophet's ﷺ wives sometimes cut their hair very short.

> **Abu Salamah ibn Abd al-Rahman narrated that: "The wives of the Prophet ﷺ used to cut their hair until it came just below their ears."**
> **- [Sahih Muslim]**

However, it is Haraam for women to shave it all off unless it is a necessity.

> **Ali ﷺ narrated that: "The prophet ﷺ prohibited women from shaving their heads." - [At-Tirmidhi]**

Even though it is Halaal to cut your hair, you must be careful and have a professional, or someone who knows how to do it properly, cut your hair. It is easy to unevenly cut and ruin your hair by mistake on your own. Then you'll have to wait many months or years for it to grow out evenly again.

DYING THE HAIR JET BLACK

It is Haraam for Muslims to dye their hair jet black. This is to avoid tricking someone about your natural hair color. Dyeing the hair black is a sin that can prevent you from Jannah.

> **Abdullah ibn Abbaas narrated that the Prophet ﷺ said: "At the end of time there will be people who will use this black dye like the crops of doves who will not experience the fragrance of Paradise." - [Abu Dawood]**

However, it is Halaal, healthy, and the Sunnah to dye your hair with Henna. Henna is good for getting rid of dandruff, growing your hair, and keeping your hair and scalp strong and healthy. But be sure you are using pure Henna and not chemical Henna dye. This is not good for your hair, and is just as bad as unnatural chemical dyes.

WEARING AND ADDING HUMAN OR SYNTHETIC HAIR TO YOUR OWN

It is Haraam to take human hair and apply it to your own. This includes wigs, weaves, braiding hair, and any hair pieces that look like real hair. Not only is is Haraam to wear, but also to install for others, sell in your store, or even to donate and sell your own hair.

> **Abdullaah narrated that: "The Prophet ﷺ has cursed the woman who adds some false hair and the woman who asks for it, the woman who tattoos and the woman who asks for it. "- [Abu Dawood]**

However, using yarn and wool to braid or twist into your hair is Halaal according to some scholars, as long as it is not black, and it must be a color that is obviously different from your own. This is to avoid tricking people about your true hair color and length. Because there is a difference of opinion on the subject, ask your parents which opinion they follow and never stop learning about Islaam, so you can make your own informed decision one day, Insha Allaah.

SKINCARE AND NATURAL BEAUTY

AlHamdulillaah, Allaah blessed you to be a girl. He created you uniquely beautiful, from your hair to your toes, you were fashioned with care. We all come in different shapes, sizes, skin tones, hair types, and facial features; all have their own strengths, and are truly beautiful when properly taken care of.

In Islaam, women are encouraged to take care of themselves. As long as you are not excessive in your pursuit of beauty, putting effort into your looks is a fun and healthy habit. As you grow older, your physical appearance might matter more to you than it once did. It is natural to compare yourself to your age group and want to be as pretty as those around you, but remember, dear reader, that comparison is the thief of joy, and comparing to the point of negative feelings is not healthy at all.

From the beginning of Puberty until your early twenties, your body is on a journey growing into an adult one—your features are changing, and you'll soon be searching for your own style. As your features begin to settle, you'll learn what suits you best and what makes you feel the most beautiful. Until you figure it out, this chapter is all about caring for your natural face and bringing out the best of it.

EXCESSIVELY CHASING BEAUTY

Before learning about skincare and bringing out your natural features, it's important to remember that you should not be excessive in your pursuit of beauty.

SIGNS YOU'RE TAKING BEAUTY TOO FAR

- Feeling angry or sad about how your body parts and facial features look

- Feeling angry, sad, jealous, or ugly when you see other beautiful people

- Wanting to or getting plastic surgery for things that aren't a deformity

Beware! Choosing beauty standards over Allaah's commands is a great sin!

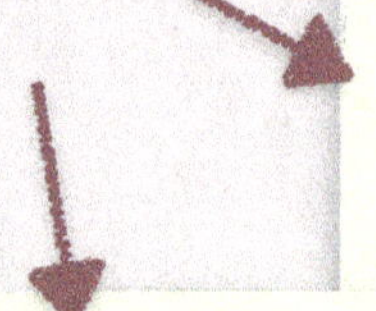

- Feeling sad, ugly, or anxious when you can't wear makeup

- Having an extensive daily beauty routine that does not allow you to be on time for school and work

- Skipping prayers or praying late because you don't want to take off your makeup, nail polish, skincare products, or ruin your hair

- Choosing hairstyles and beauty products that invalidate your wudhoo and worship

- Choosing not to wear proper hijaab because the thought of not meeting your beauty standard makes you feel sad, ugly, anxious, angry, or jealous

- To meet body goals, you go without eating or over exercise, feeling guilty, angry, or ashamed if you don't keep up with your extreme diet or schedule

Of course it's great to care about how you look and have a beauty routine and personal style, but if it's causing you bodily harm, making you feel anxious or ugly when you can't do it, or causing you to leave off wearing hijaab correctly and disobey Allaah, you are taking it too far and are now committing a sin!

> **"And whoever disobeys Allaah and His Messenger and transgresses His limits - He will put him into the Fire to abide eternally therein, and he will have a humiliating punishment." - [Quraan, 4:14]**

You must always remember that outer beauty means nothing without good character and putting Allaah first. If you ignore Allaah's commands, and treat others badly, then you will always be ugly, no matter how pretty you are on the outside.

HAVING INSECURITIES

I'll let you in on a little secret: During Puberty, everyone is insecure about something.

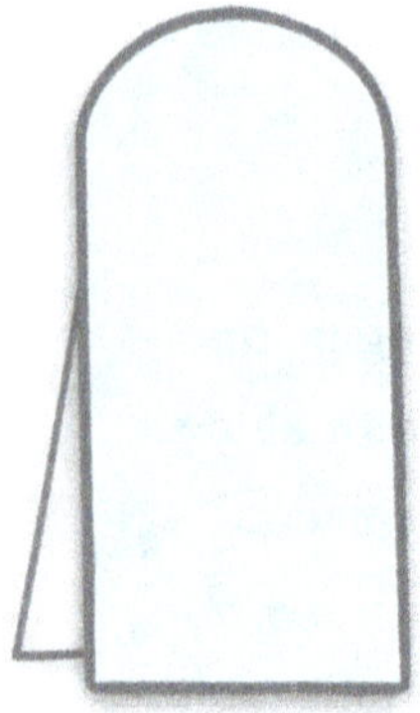

This is the point in life where you watch your body shift into something new. While some might welcome this change with open arms, it's strange and scary for others. It's normal to be uncomfortable with growing body hair, budding breasts, and new curves, or to feel you aren't growing as fast or shapely as you'd like. Saying goodbye to old clothes, and having to fully cover isn't so easy to do overnight. And seeing your face change in the mirror can be a weird feeling, even if you like the way it's turning out. Sometimes it's hard seeing yourself become a new person, especially if it isn't in the way you preferred or expected; but it's human nature, and no one can escape it. Everyone is changing, and that's a good thing! Allaah created us to evolve overtime, your body is turning out exactly how He decided it to be.

Allaah made you unique and one of a kind. You are just as you should be. You are Beautiful. Never let anyone tell you otherwise—even yourself!

You should never feel sad, anxious, or nervous about what others think about your looks. **If they can't accept Allaah's creation, shame on them!** Having a few insecurities is completely normal, but never allow them to control your life. You are in charge of how you think and act. (If your insecurities are controlling your life, turn back to page 127 about changing your thoughts for anxiety. The same method can be used to get rid of most insecurities). Usually, if you find something unattractive about yourself, there are ways to improve it, style it, or draw attention to the features you love most to make them less noticeable. **Never resort to hating the body Allaah has given you, putting yourself down, or thinking you aren't good enough based on the way you were born.**

Choose to be grateful for your body, your face, and who you are. When bad thoughts about your looks come, choose to drown out those thoughts with good ones.

Remember, it's only Shaytaan trying to put you down. Don't let him win! After all, he is going to the Hellfire, and you are better than him! Don't let the whispers of a cursed Jinn overtake you; Allaah raised you higher than that, and you should act like it.

SKIN DO'S AND DON'TS

Did you know that your skin is actually your body's largest organ? When you look at it that way, it's no wonder you should be taking care of it. During Puberty, you may have acne that clears and reappears over the years. Things like blackheads, whiteheads, and a pimple here and there are totally normal, and **you should only be worried if the pimples look like a rash, are overly painful and sensitive, or come in large clusters on your face.** In cases like that, you should see a dermatologist (a skin, hair, and nails doctor), and they will prescribe a treatment plan that is right for you.

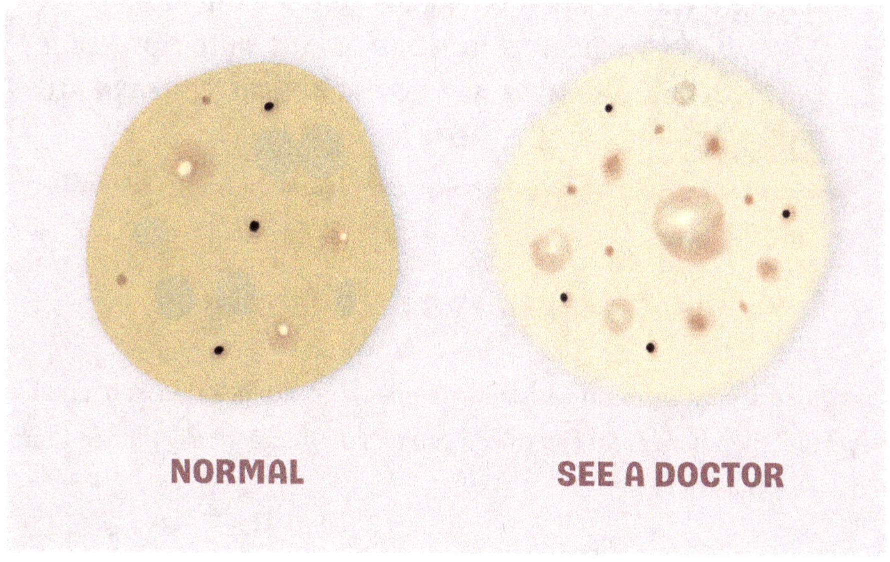

But if you have fairly normal skin with a few pimples on your cheeks or forehead, a blackhead here and there, and whiteheads on your nose or chin, then there isn't anything to worry about. Your skin will likely clear up for good after your Puberty years are over. Until then, as long as you follow these do's and don'ts, your skin should stay fairly clear and won't flare up as much in the first place.

Another thing to remember is that **if you are stressed and end up eating foods that make you feel bad or you are on your menses, then your acne might get worse,** but no worries, it's only temporary and will probably clear up on its own in a few days.

<table>
<tr><td>**DO:**</td><td>**DON'T:**</td></tr>
<tr><td>✓ Wash face with cold water</td><td>✗ Touch your face</td></tr>
<tr><td>✓ Moisturize</td><td>✗ Use products with Fragrance in them</td></tr>
<tr><td>✓ Drink lots of water</td><td>✗ Eat foods that make you feel bad</td></tr>
<tr><td>✓ Wear sunscreen</td><td>✗ Leave shampoo & conditioner on skin</td></tr>
</table>

WANT TO KNOW ABOUT THE DO'S AND DON'TS IN MORE DETAIL? PULL OUT YOUR CAMERA APP AND SCAN HERE TO LEARN ALL ABOUT THEM!

WHAT SHOULD I DO IF I BREAK OUT?

If you suddenly wake up with new pimples that are irritated, red, and an eyesore, then here are a few things you can do to drastically reduce them in a few hours or less.

ICE IT

Get some ice and put it in a thin cloth so you can hold onto it. Put the ice on the pimple or red spot for 3-5 minutes; this should reduce the redness and swelling, and it can be done over and over to keep it from getting worse throughout the day.

USE DILUTED TEA TREE OIL AS A SPOT TREATMENT

Take a drop of tea tree oil and mix it with some Vaseline, olive, or coconut oil. Gently rub it onto the pimple, and it will pull out the bacteria and greatly reduce or completely get rid of the pimple by the end of the day. **DO NOT use tea tree oil on its own, as it is too strong to be used raw and can cause a rash.**

USE A SHEET MASK

You can buy sheet masks at your local drugstore, supermarket, or beauty supply store. **Look for the ones that are exfoliating, hydrating, anti-inflammatory, and/or cleansing.** The specific ingredients you should look for are **benzoyl peroxide, Salicylic acid,** and **Sulfur.** These work to get rid of bacteria, unclog pores, and reduce redness and inflammation. Use the mask as instructed on the packaging, and **always look up reviews on the product before buying and using it on your own skin.**

BUY AN OVER-THE-COUNTER SPOT TREATMENT

At your local drugstore, you can ask for an acne spot treatment. These are usually inexpensive and can work pretty well. Use them as instructed on the packaging, and **always look up reviews of the product before buying and using it on your skin.**

As long as you follow the dos and don'ts as well as these steps for managing breakouts, your skin should be good to go. There isn't much else that is necessary unless you prefer it or have a specific problem you would like to get rid of, like hyperpigmentation or hormonal acne.

However, some girls are looking to have extra silky, smooth, clear, and hydrated skin. To achieve this, you will need to have a consistent skincare routine that you follow every day. Some people do their routine twice a day, once in the morning and again at night, but **if you only have time to do it once, do it at night because nighttime is when your skin naturally goes into repair mode.**

As Muslims, we must offer wudhoo multiple times a day. **If your face is too oily from the skincare products, it blocks the water from touching your skin, which invalidates your wudhoo.** Be sure to get into wudhoo before doing your skincare routine in the morning, and then wait to do your night routine until you have prayed all your prayers for the day.

Always do your skincare routine after your shower. This way, the conditioner and shampoo are fully off your face, and the steam from the hot shower helps open up your pores, allowing the skincare products to absorb more effectively into your skin.

WHAT IS MY SKIN TYPE?

Something that may change your skincare routine or make you add or avoid certain products is the type of skin you naturally have. There are five types of skin overall.

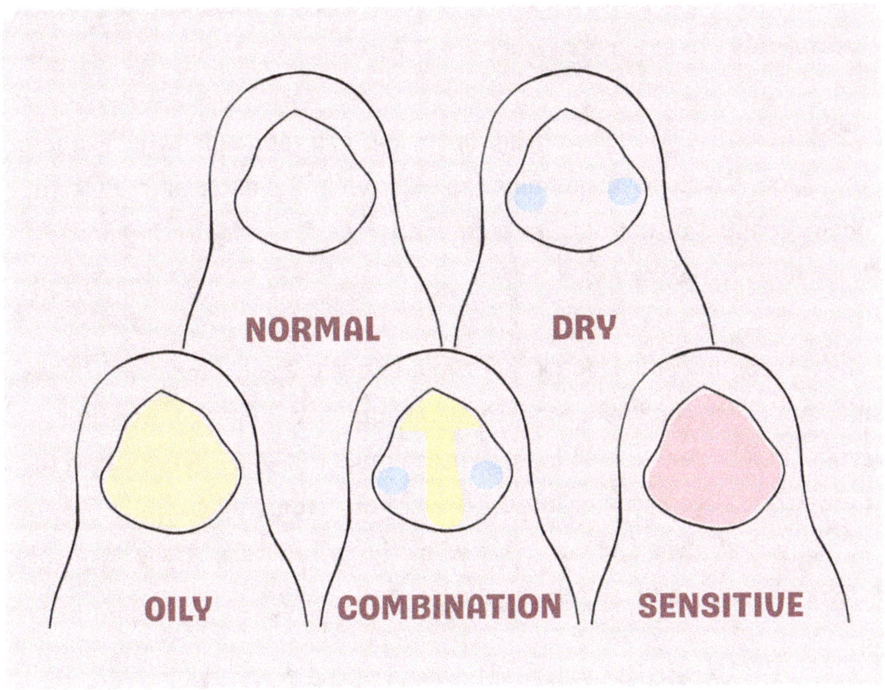

NORMAL - The normal skin type has a regular texture, isn't dry or oily, and doesn't really need any extra care. You can probably follow any simple skincare routine without needing to treat anything specific.

DRY - This skin type means your skin is rough, looks dry, and can have little cracks. Your skin can easily become ashy or itchy, and you may be prone to redness or eczema (an inflamed skin condition). **For dry skin, make sure your skincare routine is extra moisturizing. This will help soothe and nourish your skin, reducing those dry spots and itchiness.**

OILY - In the hair follicles of your skin, there are glands that produce something called Sebum. Sebum is an oily substance your body makes to keep your skin moisturized. If you have an oily skin type, this means there is an overproduction of sebum all over your face, which can make your face look shiny and break out often. **For oily skin, avoid skincare products that are oil-based and search for water-based products instead, and be careful not to over moisturize.**

COMBINATION - Your forehead, nose, and chin are called the T-zone of your face. If you have combination skin, your T-zone is oily, while your cheeks are dry or normal. **For combination skin, use hydrating products and avoid oil-based ones.**

SENSITIVE - Sensitive skin is self-explanatory. It easily becomes irritated, red, and itchy and is prone to breakouts and negative reactions to products. **For sensitive skin, moisturize regularly, and always patch test products before applying them all over your face. Be careful with what you buy, and always check reviews of the products to make sure they won't trigger a bad reaction on your skin.**

A SIMPLE DAILY SKINCARE ROUTINE

Here is a simple, six-step skincare routine that will work for most skin types and should be easy to maintain. Always check the reviews for each product to be sure they really work before buying, and remember that expensive isn't always better. Use affordable brands so you can keep up with your skincare routine.

1. **CLEANSE**
2. **ICE/JADE ROLL FACE**
3. **VITIMAIN C SERUM**
4. **MOISTURIZE**
5. **SUNSCREEN**
6. **LIP BALM/CHAPSTICK**

STEP ONE - CLEANSE

The first step in your skincare routine is to cleanse your face. This is to get off all the dirt, sweat, bacteria, and dead skin that has built up overnight or during the day. It gently exfoliates and unclogs your pores, giving you a clean and fresh slate to work with.

Avoid cleansers with **fragrances** and **parabens**. Look for specific ingredients like **salicylic acid** (which reduces redness and swelling) and **glycerin** (which hydrates and softens skin).

Some say retinol is also beneficial, but if you are a young girl, it is an unnecessary ingredient. Retinol increases skin cell production, renewing the skin and making it tight and rejuvenated. This is something your skin naturally and quickly does when you are young, which is why you don't usually see people under twenty-five with wrinkles or loose skin.

STEP TWO - ICE OR JADE ROLL YOUR FACE

Icing your face reduces acne, redness, puffiness, swelling, oiliness, and wrinkles. It closes your pores, keeping your skin looking tight, fresh, glowing, and naturally blushed. To ice your face, you can use a piece of ice wrapped in a thin cloth to gently rub on your skin until completely melted, or a jade roller, which can be kept in the freezer until ready for use.

STEP THREE - VITAMIN C SERUM

Vitamin C serum hydrates your skin, evens it out, reduces red spots, hyperpigmentation (spots or patches of skin that are darker brown, black, gray, or red and come from sun damage, acne, or hormonal imbalance), and dark spots, and protects against sun damage and wrinkles. **You will have to use this consistently for four to five months to see results on your dark spots.**

Keep in mind that hyperpigmentation generally takes six months to a year to completely disappear, and only then after being consistent in caring for it every day.

Look for the ingredient **ascorbic acid** (or l-ascorbic acid, which is the same thing); otherwise, the serum is useless. Also, **be sure it has a 10-20% concentration so it can soak into your skin.**

STEP FOUR - MOISTURIZE

Moisturizer hydrates your skin, soothes redness and inflammation, prevents skin issues, improves skin texture, and hides blemishes. This is what gives you a clean, moist look if you're going for glowing skin.

You can use a thin layer of shea butter, cocoa butter, or coconut oil as a moisturizer if you like natural ingredients, or do not want to buy a chemical one. Vaseline is also a good one. These usually work better as moisturizers than what is sold as such, and a little goes a long way.

If you are buying a moisturizer made in stores, look for one with **Hyaluronic acid**. This is a very hydrating ingredient that makes moisturizers do their job.

STEP FIVE - SUNSCREEN

If you're doing this routine in the morning, your fifth step should be sunscreen, but at night, this step should be skipped since you won't be in the sun.

Sunscreen protects your skin from UV radiation, which your skin absorbs from the sun. Sunscreen can also prevent skin cancer in some cases since it creates a barrier between your skin and UV radiation.

Finally, sunscreen protects you from age spots, hyperpigmentation, premature wrinkles, and sun damage. **It is a myth that you don't need sunscreen if your skin is darker;** perhaps the sun damage is less visible than on lighter skin, but it still happens nonetheless.

Look for sunscreen with an SPF of 30 or higher. This means higher protection from UV rays, but **check the reviews to make sure it won't leave a white cast on your face.**

STEP SIX - LIP BALM OR CHAPSTICK

Finally, use a chapstick or lip balm to keep your lips soft and moisturized. Dry, cracked lips don't look good on anyone, so always make sure to use this, even if you don't follow a skincare routine.

Look for chapsticks with shea butter, cocoa butter, jojoba, or honey in them. Vaseline, Carmex, and Auquaphor are brands known for having the best chapsticks. These moisturize and nourish your lips very well. Avoid lip balms with **fragrance, parabens,** and **alcohol,** as these dry out and irritate your lips.

<h1 style="text-align:center">WEEKLY EXTRAS</h1>

EXFOLIATE - Once or twice a week, you should exfoliate your skin with a face scrub or chemical exfoliator. This will get rid of dead skin cells, unclog pores, prevent breakouts, and give you a smooth, glowing look. Exfoliating should not be done every day since it can be harsh on the skin and cause dark spots and irritation.

SHEET MASK - Between 1-3 times a week, you should wear a sheet mask to soothe, hydrate, and make your skin glow.

HOW CAN I LOOK GOOD WITHOUT MAKEUP?

Wearing Makeup is Halaal, and as long as your parents approve, you can experiment and try out looks to enhance and beautify your features. **However, it is Haraam to wear makeup in front of non-Mahram men** since that is beautification which is not naturally a part of your face. In the ayah of hijaab, it is mentioned that this should not be done.

> **"...that they should not display their beauty and ornaments except what must ordinarily appear thereof..." - [Quraan 24:31]**

Not wearing makeup outside certainly doesn't mean you can't look good. A lot of current makeup trends are used to give the illusion that someone naturally has clear skin, an even skin tone, shapely brows, long lashes, a youthful blush, and plump lips. With some effort, you can achieve these things naturally, and if you like to wear makeup at the right times, by following these steps, you will have a better base to work with.

KEEP GOOD HYGIENE AND SMELL GOOD

You might be rolling your eyes on this one, but **you must be clean before you can be beautiful.** It doesn't matter if you're the most gorgeous woman to ever walk this earth. If you smell bad, you look bad. All the effort you put into your outfit, hair, and face makes no difference when your odor is offending others or making people avoid you.

Good hygiene not only assures you are smelling good, but feeling good too! How can you enjoy looking pretty while your skin is itching from not being washed or your breath is stinky from not brushing your teeth? Being clean will give you the confidence to smile and interact with others. A clean body gives you a fresh feel that will certainly boost your mood and self-esteem, Insha Allaah.

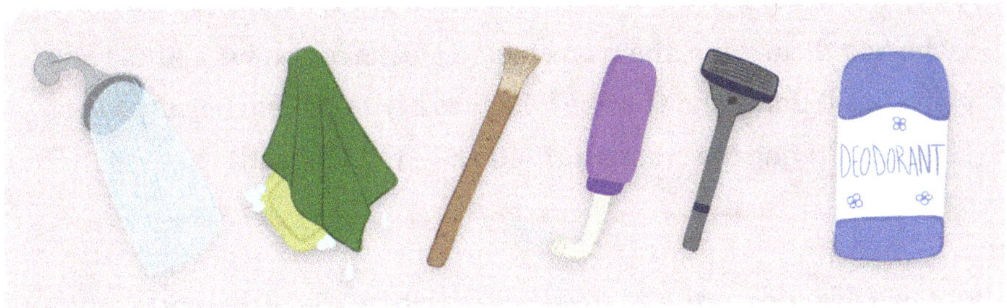

SKINCARE

Clear skin is the basis of being a natural beauty. Even if they don't say it, people notice when your skin is glowing and soft. A lot of girls only do makeup to hide the problems they have from a lack of skin care, such as uneven skin tone, dark spots, or acne. If you get rid of those things with care and have clear, supple, radiant skin, you'll already be a step ahead of the rest.

GROW YOUR EYEBROWS AND LASHES

Your eyebrows are a defining feature of your face. They're like natural frames for your eyes, and changing them changes your entire facial appearance. Your eyebrows are one of the main things that make your face look like your face. Muslims cannot alter their bodies in ways that change the way Allaah created us. This is why plucking and shaving eyebrow hairs is Haraam.

> 'Abd-Allaah ibn Mas'ud ﷺ said: "I heard the Messenger of Allaah ﷺ say, 'Allaah has cursed the woman who does tattoos and the one who has them done, the woman who plucks eyebrows and the one who has it done, and the one who files her teeth for the purpose of beauty, altering the creation of Allaah.'" - [al-Bukhaari]

But taking care of your eyebrows has nothing to do with removing them. **Everyday, you should brush them with a clean mascara wand (make sure there is no product on it or else it is considered makeup) for a groomed and maintained look.** If you have a unibrow, it is Halaal to get rid of the connecting hairs and nothing else, as that is considered extra body hair which can be removed. If your eyebrows are sparse and thin, and you'd like to grow them out, **thoroughly massage castor oil into your brows before bed, or use a growth serum which can be store-bought or homemade.**

Long eyelashes are a sign of youthfulness and give a more feminine appearance. Noticeably lengthy lashes are something people will certainly compliment you for if you have them. No worries if your lashes are short; you can grow them out the same way you do with eyebrows. Just use your homemade or store-bought eyebrow and lash serum and thoroughly apply it to your lashes every night. To groom your lashes, brush them out with a clean mascara wand everyday (make sure there is no product on it, or else it is considered makeup).

DIY EYEBROW/EYELASH GROWTH SERUM

1. Castor oil (2 tbsp)
2. Coconut oil (1 tbsp)
3. Lavender essential oil (5-10 drops)
4. Massage into hairs with fingers or a clean mascara wand
5. Let it soak in for 30 minutes before washing off, or keep on overnight

If you would rather buy a eyebrow and lash-growing serum, check the reviews to be sure it works before purchasing.

ICE YOUR EYES

Having eye bags and dark circles makes you look older and tired. The more awake and healthy your eyes look, the more they brighten up your face and make you look youthful and pretty. If you don't follow the skincare routine mentioned earlier, at least ice your eyes to decrease puffiness, redness, eye bags, and dark circles. Just place some ice in a thin cloth and hold it to each eye for a minute or so.

MASSAGE YOUR CHEEKS

When people do makeup, they are often looking for a youthful, flustered appearance. To do this, a major step in most makeup routines is blush. For a natural blush that will last you from morning to late afternoon, massage your cheeks with your fingers for a full minute. This will get your blood pumping in that area and give a cute tint to your face.

WHITEN YOUR TEETH

If your teeth are yellow and have things stuck in them, just know that people will certainly notice. **Brush your teeth 2-3 times a day and stay away from foods that might stain them, like coffee, curry, and fruit juices. You can use teeth whitening strips or a mix of baking soda and lemon juice as toothpaste for an instant result with natural ingredients.**

A Miswak will also whiten your teeth as well as make them stronger because of the herbs it is naturally infused with. A bright smile is a noticeable quality that will definitely make you sparkle, so be sure to smile often and let your teeth shine Insha Allaah!

LIP CARE

There is nothing that will ruin a look more than having crusty lips. **Gently exfoliate and clean your lips with a washcloth, toothbrush, or lip scrub once or twice a week.** You can get a store-bought lip scrub, or make one at home.

DIY LIP SCRUB

1. Olive oil or honey (1 tsp)
2. Sugar (2 tsp)
3. Mix until sugar is dissolved and rub it into your lips
4. Let it sit for 5-10 minutes
5. Wash off with cold water
6. Make sure to moisturize or else this could be too harsh on your lips

To keep them soft, hydrated, and healthy, use Vaseline, Carmex, or Aquaphor. Do not use tinted, colored, or glossy lip balms/chapsticks or else it is considered makeup).

Some girls have hyperpigmentation on their lips, which makes them appear dark instead of a pink or reddish color. This is totally normal and natural, but if you'd like your lips to be lighter, you can purchase a turmeric lip scrub or make one yourself. Use as instructed on the packaging, and your lips should brighten into their natural pinkish-reddish tone.

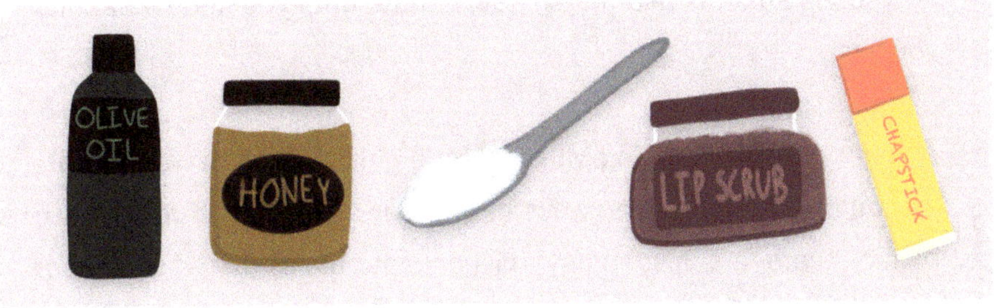

WEAR HENNA

It is the Sunnah to adorn your skin and nails with Henna. Having your nails dyed and your skin stained with decorative designs is a noticeable detail that gives an alluring, feminine vibe to your appearance. You don't have to wait for Eid to give yourself beautiful designs, keep up with your Henna on the weekly for that extra special flair.

Aisha narrated that: "A woman made a sign from behind a curtain to indicate that she had a letter for the Messenger of Allaah ﷺ. The Prophet ﷺ closed his hand, saying: 'I do not know this is a man's or a woman's hand'. She said: 'No, a woman'. He said: 'If you were a woman, you would make a difference to your nails, meaning with henna'". - [Abu Dawood]

PROPER HIJAAB AND DRESSING YOUR BEST

Now that you're clean and know how to care for your hair and skin, it's time to learn how to dress. The way you dress is a representation of you. When in the company of your family, friends, and other people, you do not have to wear hijaab in front of them; you can dress in almost any style you like. Don't be afraid to try new aesthetics and mix and match your outfits until you find what suits you best.

A major part of becoming Mukallaf for a girl is having to wear hijaab. Although there are many ways to let your style show through with hijaab, there are also many misconceptions as to what proper covering actually is.

In this chapter, you will learn how to dress well no matter what style you prefer and get to the bottom of how to cover according to the Quraan and Sunnah.

COVERING YOUR AWRAH

Before choosing what to wear, dear reader, there is something you must consider. Does this outfit cover your Awrah? **Awrah means nakedness. Your Awrah is your private parts + what Allaah and the Prophet ﷺ told us to cover. It is Haraam for others to see your Awrah.** Even inside the house in front of family, there are body parts that are considered Awrah.

> **"Oh children of Adam! We have provided for you clothing to cover your nakedness and as an adornment..." - [Quraan, 7:26]**

Your Awrah in front of Mahram men is from chest to knees. **Mahram men are men in your family who you cannot marry.** These include your father, grandfathers, brothers, sons, uncles, nephews, and boys who have not become mukallaf yet.

Whether they are family or not, your Awrah in front of other women is between your navel and your knees. **Just because it is not mentioned, this**

does not mean your chest can be naked in front of other women. It just means that the Awrah is specifically haraam for them to see.

Ali ؓ narrated that the Messenger of Allaah ﷺ said: "Do not show your thigh, and do not look at the thigh of anyone, living or dead." - [Abu Dawood]

Ibn 'Abbaas ؓ narrated that the Prophet ﷺ said: "The thigh is 'Awrah." - [at-Tirmidhi]

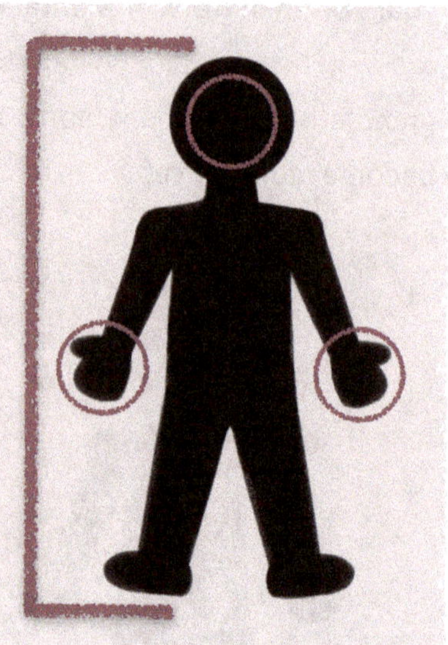

In front of men who are not Mahram for you, your Awrah is the entire body besides your hands and face. **There is a difference of opinion amongst the scholars as to whether your face (excluding the eyes) should be covered as well.** Ask your parents which opinion they follow and never stop learning about Islaam, so you can make your own informed decision one day, Insha Allaah.

WHAT IS HARAAM TO WEAR?

Before going shopping, even for inside clothes, you must remember the things to avoid that are Haraam for Muslims to wear.

CLOTHES WITH IMAGES OF FACES, SHIRK SYMBOLS, AND PHRASES THAT ENCOURAGE HARAAM

In Islaam, we are taught that the angels do not enter the house that contains a dog and images of faces, as mentioned in this Hadeeth:

The Prophet ﷺ said: "The angels do not enter a house in which there is a dog or pictures." - [al- Bukhaari]

In this Hadeeth, "pictures" are referring to images, idols, or art made by a human, depicting living beings (humans or animals). This is because photos of living things are often used as idols, and the people who are image makers of living humans and animals are committing a grave sin.

With this in mind, having a shirt with an image of a human or animal with eyes and facial features is something you cannot pray with, even if it is hidden under your prayer garment, and is also keeping the angels out of your house.

It is also Haraam to wear clothing that has symbols of other religions or Haraam actions on it, such as a cross, the star of David, Zodiac symbols, or phrases that encourage Haraam, such as 'See you in Hell'.

CLOTHING OF THE DISBELIEVERS

Clothing that represents a different religion, such as a cross necklace, nun outfit, or a sikh turban, is Haraam in Islaam, as we are not supposed to wear clothing that is exclusively for the disbelievers.

MEN'S CLOTHING

In Islaam, it is Haraam for men to dress like women and women to dress like men. In fact, the Prophet ﷺ cursed the people who cross-dress.

The way you dress represents who you are on the inside, not just to others but to your mind as well. If you wear clothes that are specifically made for men, such as thoubs, kuffis, boxer briefs, certain pants, hats, suits, and culturally male clothing, you are confusing your mind about who you really are without meaning to do so.

Doing this publicly also normalizes a sinful act that is harmful to society and should never be done. The person who does this is in danger of being cursed and should stop right away, ask forgiveness, and ask Allaah to make their mind strong so they never do it again.

FINDING THE RIGHT BRA

As your body develops, so will your breasts, which will continue to grow and change until you are twenty-five years old, Insha Allaah.

Some girls will be flat-chested, either for a little while or even as adults. Some girls will have small, medium, or different-sized breasts, and others will develop early and have large breasts either from a young age or later on as they continue to grow. No matter what size chest you develop, be thankful to Allaah and care for them by practicing good eating habits to keep them healthy along with the rest of your body.

A part of caring for your breasts is the bra you choose to wear. A bra is an undergarment that gives your breasts support and keeps them comfortable and cozy throughout the day. Without a bra, you may find your chest sticking out through your clothes, getting in the way of physical activities such as running and exercise, or needing support to keep them in place for an outfit or activity.

If you need a bra, there are different types to choose from for different reasons, but always remember to choose for comfort first. Your undergarments should be there for support and comfort, not to make you itchy, irritated, confined, or uncomfortable.

HOW TO FIND YOUR BRA SIZE

With a measuring tape, **measure the inches around your bust (at nipple level) and write it down.** Then, **measure the inches around your ribs (where the bra band would be under your breasts).** Your rib measurement will equal a rib number, as shown in the chart below.

Next, **subtract the rib number you get on that chart from the bust measurement you wrote down earlier**, and you will be left with a number from 0-4. Each number equals a letter, as shown on the chart below; that letter is your cup size.

Your bra size is your rib number and cup letter put together, for example: 34B.

Rib number: **Cup size:**

22-23 = 28   0 = AA   Bust measurement
24-25 = 30   1 = A   Rib measurement
26-27 = 32   2 = B
28-29 = 34   3 = C
30-31 = 36   4 = D

Bust measurement - Rib number = Cup size

Rib number + Cup size = Bra size

TYPES OF BRAS

TRAINING BRAS

Training bras look like half tank tops with an elastic band at the bottom to keep them secure. They have little to no padding and are used to help you get used to wearing a full bra. They are often worn when your breasts first start to develop so you can feel comfortable in this first stage of growth, and so your initial nipple protrusions aren't visible to others.

SOFT BRAS

Soft bras give gentle support with soft fabric and little padding. This bra will not keep your breasts in place but will allow them to be comfortable under your clothes with minimal support.

CUP BRAS

Cup bras are structured and not as bendable and gentle as soft bras. They give your breasts a lot of support and an even shape under your clothes. Cup bras are known to be the most restricting and sometimes uncomfortable because of the underwire they often come with.

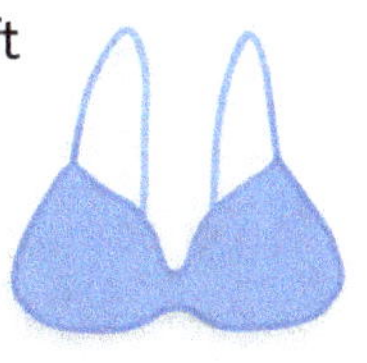

SPORTS BRAS

Sports bras gently but firmly hold your breasts in place and give them an even shape under your clothing. These are known to be one of the most comfortable options, as they snuggly fit without having irritating underwire or materials. As said in the name, these bras are made specifically for sports so your breasts don't move around while running, jumping, skipping, playing, etc.

BANDEAU BRAS

Bandeau bras, **also called tube or strapless bras,** have no straps and gently but firmly wrap around your breast for comfort and support. They are usually worn when you don't want your straps to show through an outfit or would rather not have straps for comfort reasons.

Do not leave uncomfortable straps to irritate you, as they can cause bruises and neck and shoulder pain. If they are too tight, loosen them right away. If they are too loose and keep falling down without giving your chest support, tighten them. If one of your breasts is smaller or needs more support than the other, tighten the strap on that side only. Although bras are important for daily activity, comfort, and dressing, **they should not be worn during the night.** It is important that your breasts get a break from restrictive clothing while sleeping; this way they can be free to rest and rejuvenate like the rest of your body.

TAKING CARE OF YOUR CLOTHES

The way you dress is a representation of who you are. If your clothes are wrinkled, smelly, and have holes in them, people will think you are dirty, lazy, or have no manners or class. Even though you should not judge a person based on clothing alone, it is certainly the first thing people notice when they meet you for the first time.

It is human nature to form opinions about someone based on your first impression of them. Of course, it's never okay to treat anyone badly, but not everyone will have good manners and think well of you despite a bad first impression.

Even inside your home, you should not be smelly, as your body odor can offend your family. Your clothes should not be wrinkly or have holes, as it is a sign you do not take care of yourself, which can make your brain think negatively about yourself without consciously meaning to.

You do not have to be financially wealthy to take care of your clothes, just be careful not to damage the clothes your parents give you, and implement these tips to care for them.

AVOID ROUGHHOUSING

At a certain age, playing rough and not caring about your clothes is acceptable, but as you get older, you must learn to be calm and care for the blessings Allaah has given you, including your clothing. Running, biking, tripping, and falling are all actions that could lead to ripped and dirty clothes.

You must be very careful when being active so that you are not reckless and needlessly damaging your property. Your parents likely spent hard-earned money to make sure you are dressed well and look presentable. A part of being thankful towards them is caring for what they buy you. If you bought the clothes yourself, that's even more of a reason to care for them since you spent well-earned money and should have pride in the possessions Allaah has allowed you to get.

CHANGE CLOTHES AFTER A SHOWER

When you are done showering, either in the morning or at night, change into another clean outfit. Wearing the same thing after your body is scrubbed and cleaned puts the stink and dirt back on. This not only makes you dirty again but smelly, too. Always change into clean clothes after a shower.

WASH YOUR CLOTHES REGULARLY

After a day of dirt and sweat build-up, put your clothes in the wash before you wear them again, especially if they smell or have noticeable stains and spots on them. **Do not let the smell build up on your clothes before you finally wash them.**

However, if you've kept your clothes clean throughout the day without a buildup of sweat or smell, a stain here and there can be hand-washed instead of going into the washing machine.

HOW TO HAND WASH

1. Fill the sink, a small bucket, bowl, or basin with water
2. Add soap or clothing detergent and baking soda (if you have any)
3. Dip clothing in water and rub it against itself to remove odors and dirt
4. Rinse with clean water
5. Allow to dry before use

KEEP WITHOUT WRINKLES

If your clothes are wrinkly, it gives the appearance of low maintenance and rushed dressing. To get rid of wrinkles, sprinkle your clean clothing with a few drops of water and throw it in the dryer for ten minutes or so on a regular setting, some dryers also have a de-wrinkle setting. Another way to de-wrinkle is if you are going to be taking a hot shower, hang your outfit on the shower curtain rack with a hanger, and without getting it wet, allow the steam to unwrinkle the clothes as you wash. If you want crisp de-wrinkling and precise edges, use an iron to straighten out the clothing. Ask your parents to teach you how to use an iron, as it is a hot tool that can burn both you and the piece of clothing if you aren't careful.

DON'T PUT HOLES IN YOUR CLOTHES

There is nothing that ruins an outfit more than an unsightly hole. Be careful when you walk and play so that you do not damage your clothing, but if you do manage to get one accidentally, there is an easy sewing technique called the invisible stitch. With this, you will be able to repair holes in your clothing and keep it looking as good as new, Insha Allaah. **To learn the invisible stitch, watch a short tutorial on YouTube and follow along.**

NEATLY STORE YOUR CLOTHES

Learn how to fold your clothing neatly and place them gently on top of each other so as not to cause wrinkles, storage smells, dust, and dirt to build up while you're not wearing them. Some things, like abayas, hijaabs, dresses, and sweaters, should be hung in a closet instead of tucked away in a drawer. This will keep the clothes in good condition until you decide to wear them again, Insha Allaah.

HOW CAN I FIND MY STYLE?

As long as your Awrah depending on the situation is covered, you may dress any way you want to express yourself. Some people are girly and like frills, dresses, bows, and pink; others are casual and enjoy comfortable sweaters, baggy shirts, jeans, and the color black. Muslims come from all over the world, and some girls enjoy wearing their own cultural style of clothing most.

There are so many ways to style yourself that you don't have to choose just one. Sometimes, it takes a while to learn what clothes look good on you and which ones you prefer. Sometimes, you may like a certain outfit and it doesn't look good on you because it isn't suited for your characteristics. This is why it's so important to know your body and appreciate the way you look. It will make styling yourself so much easier and bring out the best of your beautiful features, Insha Allaah.

YOUR UNDERTONES AND COLORS THAT SUIT YOU

Have you ever had a shirt that looked good online, in the store, or on someone else, but as soon as you put it on, something about it didn't look right? It fits well, and the rest of your clothes match, but for some reason, it just looks off. Don't worry, there isn't anything wrong with you, it may just be that the color doesn't match your undertones.

Knowing your undertones is very important because that is what determines what colors look best on you, not only for clothes but for hair color, makeup, jewelry, and lighting.

Your undertone is not your overall skin color. **No matter what skin color you are, everyone has a less obvious tone within their skin that combines with their main color; this is called an undertone.** There are three types of undertones, and each has its own set of colors that wonderfully highlight the best in your skin and outfit.

Look at the veins on your wrists. Depending on what color they are is what undertone you have. If your veins are a green or olive color, you have warm undertones. If they look like a mix of blue and green, you have neutral undertones. If they look like a mix of purple or blue, you have cool undertones.

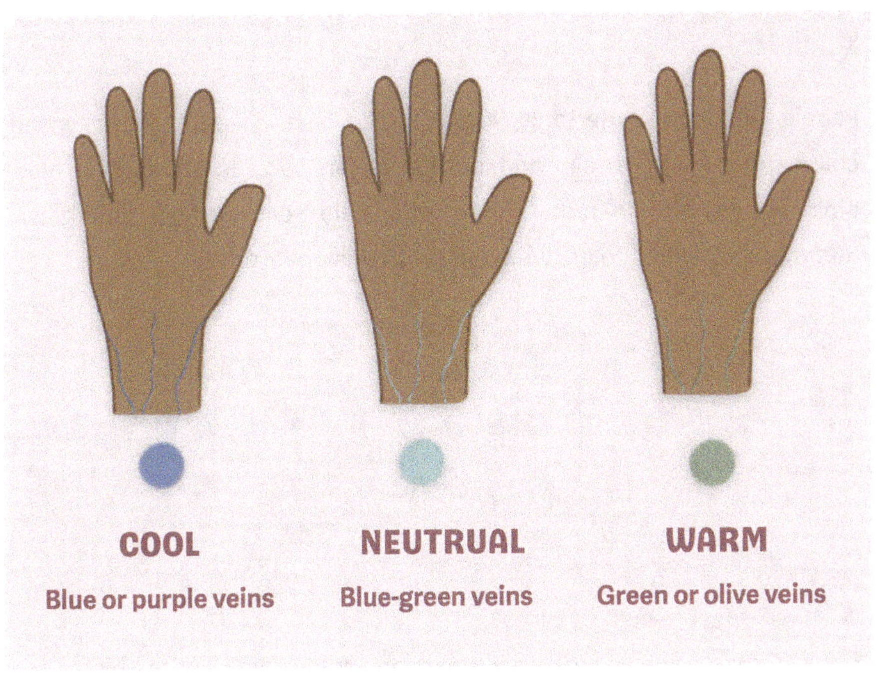

Remember that you can have any undertone with any skin color, even if you have the same skin color as someone else, you may have a completely different undertone. This is why it's always important to check which one you have for yourself.

WARM

People with warm undertones look good in yellow, gold, and warm-based colors for clothing, jewelry, and makeup. Colors such as browns, creams, gold, peach, warm reds, yellowish greens, and warm blues or purples. Spring and fall colors work best with this undertone.

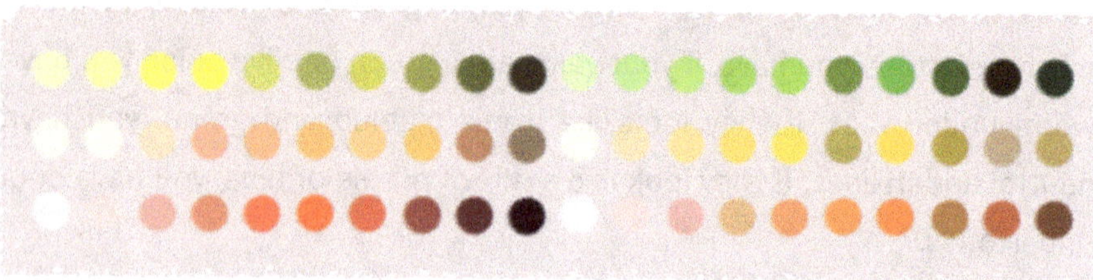

COOL

People with cool undertones look good in blue, silver, and cool-based colors for clothing, jewelry, and makeup. Colors such as white, silver, blue, pink, purple, pinkish reds, cherry reds, pale yellows, and light grays. Summer and winter colors work best with this undertone.

NEUTRAL

For this undertone, you can easily wear any color from both the warm and cool color palettes. Most will look very good on you, and you won't have to give it much thought.

Keep in mind for all undertones to stay away from colors that look exactly like your skin tone, or else they will blend in and wash you out.

LOOK UP TO GIRLS WHO LOOK LIKE YOU

When it comes to styling yourself, it is best to find others who have the same hair and body type as you to see what will look good on you specifically. Instead of looking up to celebrities and influencers who have different features than you and being disappointed if you don't pull off the same things, find others who look similar and have the same style, this way you can have a style guide based on what you really look like, and will have more success in dressing and looking your best.

This will help you see that everyone is beautiful in their own way. Accepting, loving, and caring for who you really are will make your life so much easier and your self-esteem so much higher.

You can find a style based on you by searching on Pinterest for your hair type hairstyles and body type outfits. You can even find a girl with the same facial features and skin tone as you for skincare or makeup tips and save them all to your board for reference later.

TYPES OF AESTHETICS

Your aesthetic is the type of beauty that fits your characteristics and outer style. For ideas of how to dress and what to look up to, many girls find an aesthetic they like and pick their outfits and design choices based on that. Here is a list of Aesthetics to look up on Pinterest for inspiration.

✦ Soft girl aesthetic	✦ Dark academia
✦ Balletcore	✦ Normcore
✦ Cottagecore	✦ Vintage
✦ Clean girl aesthetic	✦ Y2k
✦ Grunge aesthetic	✦ Kidcore
✦ Light academia	✦ Pastel aesthetic

If you would like the aesthetic for your own culture, you can look that up as well. There are so many to choose from, you don't have to pick just one. Mix and match until you find the style that suits you best. **Just be sure that whatever you choose does not include the clothing that is Haram for us, as mentioned before, and that it properly covers your Awrah.**

JEWELRY

Women are allowed to wear whatever jewelry they like in Islaam. However, you must be careful about the piercings you decide to get, as they may be unlawful. It's Halaal to pierce the ears and nose, but other piercings that may cause bodily harm, imitate a specific group of non-Muslims, or are on the Awrah are Haraam. For example, the stretched-out earlobe (mutilates the healthy body Allaah has given you), tongue (can cause diseases in some cases), and lip piercings (prone to infections).

Earrings, necklaces, rings, bangles, bracelets, waist beads, and anklets are all Halaal jewelry that is widely worn throughout the world. Adding Jewelry to adorn yourself makes you look a lot more feminine and brings attention to the place you wear it. **Just be careful not to wear jewelry in front of non-Mahrams, as this is Haraam because it is beautification.** If you're wearing some underneath your hijaab, as long as it is not visible in any way you can keep it on. **Make sure the jewelry you wear is made of safe materials that won't turn your skin green or cause you to break out.** Although it is pricier to get real jewelry, it is worth it to keep your skin safe. **Avoid jewelry made of nickel, brass, and plastic,** as those will irritate your skin and cause it to react negatively.

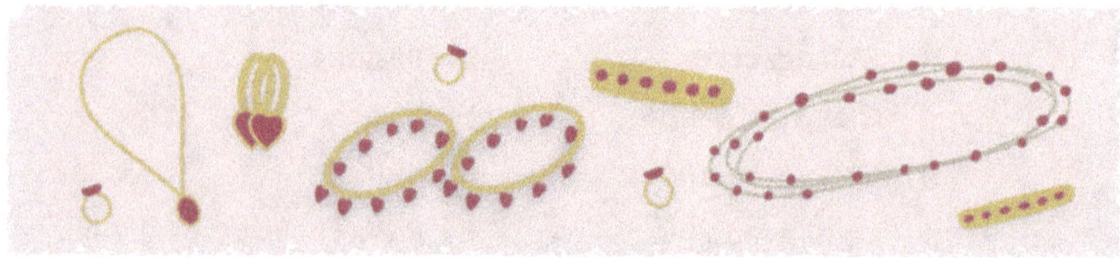

HIJAAB ACCORDING TO THE QURAAN AND SUNNAH

Finally, there is the matter of how to wear hijaab according to the Quraan and Sunnah. There are many widespread misconceptions and misinterpretations of this, especially in the West.

Once a Muslim girl hits Puberty, she must begin wearing hijaab immediately. This is a commandment from Allaah that cannot be denied. It is commonly said that wearing hijaab is a choice, which is true to an extent, as all commandments of Allaah must be chosen to act on. **However, choosing not to wear hijaab is Haraam.** It is a sin that can lead you to the Hellfire if not rectified and repented for.

Many people make up the rules of how to wear hijaab and what is okay to wear in order to make themselves feel better about not properly covering. This is Haraam, as said in these ayaat:

> "And do not describe what your tongues have lied about, saying: "This is lawful and this is forbidden," to invent lies against Allaah. Verily, those who invent lies against Allaah, will never succeed. A passing brief enjoyment (will be theirs), but they will suffer a painful torment." - [Quraan, 16:116-117]

If you are not ready to wear the hijaab at all or properly despite it being obligatory for you, this is okay to admit; but **don't lie or stretch the truth of the Quraan and Sunnah to fit the way you act when it is not what Allaah commanded.** This is a sin that will lead to torture in the hereafter. May Allaah protect us from that, Ameen!

In Suratul-Noor, we get the commandment from Allaah not to display our beauty by covering ourselves and not drawing extra attention through the way we dress and act. You don't have to do this in front of men who are

Mahram for you, such as your husband, father, father-in-law, son, stepsons, brothers, nephews, other women, specific servants, and male children who haven't hit Puberty yet.

> "And say to the believing women that they should lower their gaze and guard their private parts; that they should not display their beauty and ornaments except what must ordinarily appear thereof; that they should draw their veils over their Juyubihinna (bosoms, bodies) and not display their beauty except to their husbands, their fathers, their husbands' fathers, their sons, their husbands' sons, their brothers, or their brothers' sons or their sisters' sons, or their women or the servants whom their right hands possess, or male servants free of physical needs, or small children who have no sense of the shame of sex, and that they should not strike their feet in order to draw attention to their hidden ornaments. And oh you Believers, turn you all together towards Allaah, that you may attain Bliss." - [Quraan, 24:31]

To wear hijaab is to conceal your body shape, Awrah, and beauty. To be sure you are doing this correctly, there are eight conditions of hijaab that your clothing should meet.

ONE – THE HIJAAB MUST COVER THE ENTIRE BODY

This means that all of your Awrah must be covered. As mentioned in the earlier part of this chapter, that is your entire body besides your hands and face. There is a difference of opinion amongst the scholars as to whether your face (excluding the eyes) should be covered as well. Ask your parents which opinion they follow and go off of that. Never stop learning about Islaam, so you can make your own informed decision one day, Insha Allaah.

TWO - IT SHOULD CONCEAL EVERYTHING THAT IS UNDERNEATH IT

See-through clothing does not count as hijaab, as people can see what is underneath them, defeating the whole purpose. Your clothing should also not be such a light material that moving around makes your hijaab or abaya come up and reveal what is underneath. Pants (no matter how baggy they are) and skirts or dresses that pull in at the waist are also unacceptable, as they reveal the body shape that is underneath your clothing.

THREE - IT MUST BE LOOSE FITTING

Tight clothing that hugs your body shape, including tight-fitting abayas and skirts, are not hijaab, as it obviously shows the shape of your body and reveals the body parts underneath your clothes, which are specifically supposed to be hidden.

FOUR - IT SHOULD NOT BE PERFUMED

Smell triggers powerful feelings and hormones in human beings. Being clean is a major part of being a Muslim, however, heightening your good scent with perfume outside the home or in front of non-Mahrams is Haraam. In fact, the Prophet ﷺ referred to the woman who wears perfume and passes by a man as someone who is calling to Zinaa (which is a major sin) as said in this Hadeeth:

> **Abu Musa ﷺ narrated that: "The Prophet ﷺ said: 'If a woman puts on perfume and passes by people so that they can smell her fragrance, then she is such and such,' and he spoke sternly - meaning an adulteress." - [Abu Dawood]**

FIVE - IT SHOULD NOT BE OVERLY ADORNED

When wearing hijaab, you should avoid bright colors, patterns, bedazzlement, and designs that are made to call attention to the outfit. Jewelry outside the hijaab, such as a necklace or headdress, or allowing your earrings to stick out is also unacceptable. If you dress this way with the inner intention of getting attention and compliments, this is Haraam.

SIX - IT SHOULD NOT BE EXTRAVAGANT AND VAIN

Showing off is a major sin in Islaam. If you wear clothes that are specifically meant to show off your wealth and status with the intention of getting attention and awe from others, this is Haraam. Of course it is okay to buy expensive outfits, it just can't be with the intention of showing off, or something that calls attention to your clothing.

SEVEN - IT SHOULD NOT RESEMBLE MEN'S CLOTHING

As mentioned earlier in this chapter, it is Haraam for men to wear women's clothing and women to wear men's clothing. So do not wear kufis, thobes, certain pants, suits, and culturally men's clothing like the West African agbada, for example.

EIGHT - IT SHOULD NOT RESEMBLE NON-MUSLIM CLOTHING

Muslims have their own way of covering that comes from the Quraan and Sunnah; we do not need to copy the way non-Muslims dress since we have our own styles. Wearing a headscarf with a tight dress, baggy pants and shirt, or long sleeve sweater and jeans is not acceptable as hijaab. These are non-Muslim items of clothing that do not even conform to the conditions of hijaab. Besides the laymen's way of dressing, it is also not acceptable to dress in ways that represent other religions. For example, the outfit of a nun specifically represents Christianity and would be Haraam for a Muslim woman to wear.

HIJAAB STYLES

Now that you understand the conditions of proper covering, let's look at some examples of hijaab that go along with the Quraan and Sunnah. Keep in mind, depending on where you live, these garments can be called by different names than what's written here.

A LONG SHAYLA

A Shayla is a long rectangular or square cut of fabric that is wrapped, pinned, and tucked around the head and upper body. There are so many colors and styles of wrapping to choose from with this hijaab, but be sure it meets the conditions of hijaab, and fully covers your hair, head, neck, and chest. The shayla should go down to your waist so when you move around, you will not be exposed.

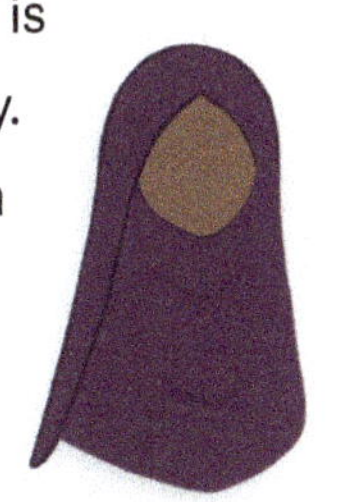

KHIMAAR

This type of hijaab is a one-piece covering that goes around the head and upper body. Sometimes the face opening comes with elastic or tie strings to keep it secure around your head; others come with built-in niqaabs so you don't have to put them on separately. A khimaar can come in many cuts, sizes, and even layers. Just be sure that yours is long enough to cover your head, hair, neck, and chest, at least. The Khimaar should go down to your waist so that when you move around, you will not be exposed.

ABAYA

This type of covering is a long-sleeved loose garment that can be opened down the middle or closed and covers the entire body from your shoulders to your feet. Abayas come in so many colors and styles, such as standard, wide, butterfly-winged, bell-sleeved, and layered. An Abaya should be worn with a shayla or khimaar that meets the conditions of hijaab. Be sure that your abaya is not tight or gathered at the waist, as this goes against the conditions of hijaab.

JILBAAB

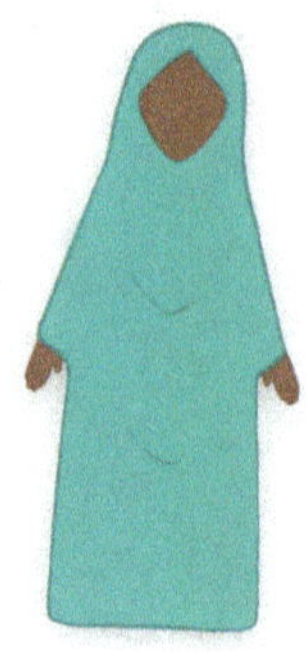

The jilbaab is a one or two-piece khimar that covers from head to toe and includes sleeves. Sometimes the face opening comes with elastic or tie strings to keep it secure around your head; others come with built-in niqaabs so you don't have to put them on separately. A one-piece jilbaab must be very long to cover your feet even when you lift your arms. A two-piece jilbaab usually has the khimaar end around your bottom or knees, and the matching skirt covers the rest.

CHADOR

Mostly worn by Iranian women, this garment covers you from head to toe but has an opening down the middle, or a wide head opening so the outfit or hijaab underneath can peek through. A chador can be paired with any hijaab, as long as your hair, head, neck, and chest are covered by it. If your chador is open down the middle, the outfit underneath needs to meet the conditions of hijaab, so you will not be exposed through the opening of the garment.

NIQAAB

The niqaab is a veil that covers your entire face besides your eyes. These can come in many styles, such as the tie back, elastic, two-layered, three-layered, a fabric strip between the eyes, a rectangle eye-opening, and an oval eye-opening. Be sure that your niqaab is not see-through as that is against the conditions of hijaab, but it should be a lightweight fabric and not restrict your breathing.

BURQA

Although most people think the burqa is only the blue garment worn by Afghani women, it is actually any garment of any color that completely covers the body from head to toe and leaves nothing to be seen; including the face, eyes, and sometimes hands. This is worn throughout the world by women who do not want any part of themselves to be visible at all.

Congratulations, dear reader! You've reached the end of this book. It's been a long journey from the beginning to now, and I hope you have greatly benefited from this work that was made just for you. Now that you've learned about hygiene, your Islaamic duties, what's going on inside, and how to style your outside, it's time to do the work and try it in real life.

You have a long way ahead of you, Insha Allaah. You'll face hardships, challenges, bad days, and bouts of low Imaan. It won't always be easy keeping on good terms with your family or friends, much less taking the time to care for yourself inside and out. Puberty is a time of ups and downs, lows and highs, being a child, and suddenly becoming an adult; but with Allaah's help and hopefully with what you've learned from this book, I know you can succeed!

You'll succeed in knowing your body and keeping it clean and strong as it blossoms into something new. You'll succeed in being a dutiful Muslim through understanding, action, and the wonderful way you connect with others. You'll succeed in healthily managing all the feelings that build up inside you, good or bad, easy to feel or hard to process. You'll succeed at cultivating the incredible beauty you are on the outside, just as much as you do within, Insha Allaah.

It may take time—maybe months, maybe years—but with the knowledge, relationships, and experiences you'll gain during these years, you will become a woman worth waiting for, Insha Allaah.

Jazaak Allaahu Khayr for getting to the end, my dearest and most wonderful reader. Asalaamu'alaykum.

ARABIC GLOSSARY

- **AlHamdulillaah** — Praise be to Allaah

- **Allaah** — The only One God Who is worthy of worship

- **Ameen** — Literally means truthful, and is said at the end of every Du'aa

- **Asalaamu'alaykum** — Peace be upon you

- **Athkaar** — Phrases that praise and remind us of Allaah.

- **Ayah** — A verse from the Quraan

- **Du'aa** — A spoken prayer to Allaah

- **Hadeeth** — A collection of authentic accounts of the Prophet ﷺ life, sayings, and daily practices

- **Hijaab** — The covering of a Muslim woman

- **Imaan** — Faith

- **Insha Allaah** — If Allaah wills

- **Jazaak Allaahu Khayr** — May Allaah reward you with goodness

- **Masha Allaah** — Allaah has willed it

- **Quraan** — The Islaamic religious text, and miraculous collection of Allaah's final message to us

- ﵁ **(Radhiallaahu Anhu)** — May Allaah be pleased with him

- ﵂ **(Radhiallaahu Anha)** — May Allaah be pleased with her

- ﷺ **(Sallaallaahu Alayhi wa sallam)** — May peace and blessings be upon him

- **Sunnah** — The daily practices and traditions of the Prophet ﷺ

JAZAAK ALLAAHU KHAYR FOR READING!

This book took a little over a year to complete from start to finish, but the idea and intention for it came a few years before the process even began. During one summer when I taught at my mothers weekend Kuttaab, I connected with an incredibly smart, lively group of middle school students. When an incident arose where hygiene needed to be discussed, I paused the usual curriculum and put a few classes together on the basics. The girls where so excited to learn about the subject that I extended the classes to Puberty, self esteem, and the importance of Islaam in our every day lives. I realized through my research, and the eager reaction from the students, how important it is that this subject be taught from an Islaamic point of view. There is so much that many Muslim parents unfortunately do not educate their daughters about, and so much in the secular teachings on Puberty that go against and leave out crucial Islaamic details which must be taught. To bring the two together in a balanced and visual way, I wrote and illustrated this book. My intention is that it greatly benefit all the young Muslimahs who are looking for guidance through this complicated stage of life. May Allaah accept this work from me, and bless my readers endlessly with good in this life and the next, ameen.

Please leave an honest review on Amazon and share your thoughts!

Amazon reviews are especially important for independent authors, as they help the book to be pushed to other readers who may enjoy and benefit from it as much as you have, Insha Allaah. I deeply appreciate your time spent reading and supporting my work. If you'd like to learn more about me and keep up with what I have in store, below is listed where you can find me online. Baarak Allaahu Feekum!

www.jennabinthakeem.com